THE IMPOSSIBLE EARL

"Marriage is the only suitable course for young women," Lord Winterton stated in his insufferably arrogant way.

"Mary Wollstonecraft called it legal prostitution," Kate retorted.

Winterton narrowed his eyes. "I doubt your parents would approve of your reading Wollstonecraft, Miss Montgomery."

"I am three and twenty and quite capable of deciding what I shall read."

"I doubt women are capable of an intelligent choice of reading material."

"I assure you your opinion is not of the slightest interest to me." Kate wheeled and headed for the door with skirts swishing in an angry hiss.

But a moment later, Winterton had caught up with her. And as Kate felt his firm grip on her arm, she knew it would be as hard to defeat his designs as change his mind. . . .

LAURA MATTHEWS was born and raised in Pittsburgh, Pennsylvania, but after attending Brown University she moved to San Francisco. Before she sat down to write her first novel, she worked for a spice company and an architectural firm, and on a psychology research project.

The Seventh Suitor

by

Laura Matthews

A SIGNET BOOK

SIGNET
Published by the Penguin Group
Penguin Books USA Inc., 375 Hudson Street,
New York, New York 10014, U.S.A.
Penguin Books Ltd, 27 Wrights Lane,
London W8 5TZ, England
Penguin Books Australia Ltd, Ringwood,
Victoria, Australia
Penguin Books Canada Ltd, 2801 John Street,
Markham, Ontario, Canada L3R 1B4
Penguin Books (N.Z.) Ltd, 182-190 Wairau Road,
Auckland 10, New Zealand

Penguin Books Ltd, Registered Offices:
Harmondsworth, Middlesex, England

Published by Signet, an imprint of New American Library,
a division of Penguin Books USA Inc.

First Signet Printing, August, 1991
10 9 8 7 6 5 4 3 2 1

 REGISTERED TRADEMARK—MARCA REGISTRADA

Printed in the United States of America

BOOKS ARE AVAILABLE AT QUANTITY DISCOUNTS WHEN USED TO PROMOTE PRODUCTS OR
SERVICES. FOR INFORMATION PLEASE WRITE TO PREMIUM MARKETING DIVISION, PENGUIN BOOKS
USA INC., 375 HUDSON STREET, NEW YORK, NEW YORK 10014.

For Paul,
with love.

1

"I am very sensible of the honor you pay me by offering for me, Lord Norris, but I fear we should not suit," Kate told the elegant young man lounging against the mantel.

This seemed to afford the young man a certain measure of relief, for he returned her quizzing smile and replied, "Of course it shall be as you wish, Miss Montgomery. But perhaps I should list my prospects for you before you reject me so cruelly."

Kate chuckled and said, "Oh, run along, Charles. Are there more?"

"Whatever can you mean, Miss Montgomery? More what?"

"You know very well, you horrid boy, but never mind. I'm sure you have taken more than your allotted time already, what with flirting with my sister before your flattering proposal to me. She will be very annoyed with you, you know."

Lord Norris drew himself up to his full six-foot height and bent a glowering look upon her, which he was unable to sustain. Nevertheless, as his word was involved and he was unable to respond in kind, he merely murmured, "You are too kind, Miss Montgomery. I shall find my way out."

When the parlor door had closed behind him, Kate

strolled to the window, puzzled but still amused. Her sister Susan burst through the door almost immediately and cried, "Lord Norris, too? Whatever has come over all of them? Was that the last? I may never speak to him again," she finished somewhat obscurely.

"Now, Susan, try not to be vexed with Charles. It is obviously some game they are all playing and he could not very well decline to participate if Geoff and Terence did. Drat, I fear that is *not* the last. Here is his brother riding up now," she remarked, her eyes fixed on the mounted youth approaching on the carriage entry.

"Wayne? This really is too much, Kate. Why, you might have accepted one of them. How were they to know you would not?"

"You are too complimentary, Susan. I presume you find me too old and infirm for all these boys. Terence Marsh is only a year younger than I, after all, and I really cannot believe that I should make such an unappealing wife when all is said and done." Kate tossed her brown curls vigorously and attempted a demure expression.

"You are mistaking my intent, Kate. You know I did not mean . . ."

Here she was interrupted by the butler, who stiffly presented himself in the doorway and announced in a disapproving voice the Honourable Wayne Norris. Sampson did not have anything against this young person in particular, but he did not understand and could not approve the comings and goings of four of the countryside's most eligible bachelors in one afternoon. He cast a pleading look at Kate, who merely grinned exasperatedly at him.

The Honourable Wayne Norris wore a more studious air than his elder brother and looked uncomfortable in his town clothes. Whereas the others had arrived in riding jackets, buckskin breeches, and top boots, Wayne had seen fit to honor the occasion (his first proposal, after all) with his idea of London finery—a close-fitting coat of dark blue superfine, moderately high shirt points, a sparkling cravat, and buff-colored pantaloons. Even his boots must have been given a rub in the hall, for they showed not the least trace of mud. His face was flushed, and he stuttered as he greeted the young women. He alone did not know precisely where to begin; and, after stooping quickly to retrieve the gloves which fell from his nerveless hands, he looked helplessly at Kate.

Kate took pity on the young man (who must be five years my junior, she thought, somewhat annoyed) and suggested, "Did you wish a word in private with me, Wayne?"

"Y-yes. That is, if Miss Susan does not mind. I should not like to inconvenience you if you are busy."

"Not at all, Wayne," Kate sighed. Her sister departed reluctantly and made an attempt to leave the door ajar, but closed it swiftly at Kate's frown. "May I offer you some refreshment?"

"Yes. No. Thank you, but I think not today. I have come on a very important matter, Miss Kate," he intoned in his serious young voice, which threatened to break at any moment.

"Please sit down, Wayne. I feel sure you will be more comfortable."

"No, thank you, I feel it would not be appropriate, perhaps. Though I am not sure. You wouldn't mind if I stood, would you?"

"No, Wayne, if you will forgive my seating myself."

"Certainly. Of course. Yes, you must be seated. Why have I kept you standing about this way? Shameful of me." He groaned and dropped his gloves again.

"Not at all." Kate arranged herself comfortably on the blue velvet sofa, which complemented her jonquil muslin, and waited for him to speak. When he continued to stare at her, she prodded him gently. "You had something important to discuss with me, Wayne?"

"Yes. I mean, very important. I have come to ask you to marry me," he blurted, clenching his long, thin hands in an agony of despair.

"No, really? Well, Wayne, I shall answer you as I have answered the others. I am very sensible of the honor you do me by offering for me, but I fear we should not suit. There, now, it is over. I do not suppose you would be any more interested in telling me what is going forward than the others, would you?"

"I . . . I . . . I . . . Thank you, Miss Kate. I . . ."

"Really, Wayne, you are not supposed to thank a young woman for refusing you, dear boy." Kate laughed, taking the sting out of her words. "If you cannot bring yourself to tell me, I shall say no more. Thank you for calling, Wayne. Sampson will see you out," she said and turned to tug the pull with more energy than was actually necessary.

When the young man had departed in red-faced confusion, Susan again descended on her sister, more intrigued than ever. Kate shook her head perplexedly and remarked, "Really, Susan, it has come to the point of insult. I shall be the talk of the neighborhood for this day's work by those silly gudgeons. Whatever did I do to deserve this?"

"Ralph probably knows. I am sure he had no need to go to Bristol at all today. He just wished to be away when the feathers started to fly." Susan gave a jerk at her skirts as though she were shaking her brother.

"I don't doubt you are right. We shall have to await his return and see if we can get the truth from him. Though you can be sure he will not like it." Kate sat musing on the sofa and speculated, "It must have to do with the Assembly last night at the Clifton Rooms. I wonder . . ."

"Mr. Benjamin Karst to see you, Miss Montgomery," Sampson announced in even frostier accents than he had used for poor Wayne Norris. This new arrival, however, was not in the least like the shy Wayne. He strode in wearing a cheeky smile and tossing a snuff box from hand to hand. The bow he made to the sisters was exaggeratedly elegant, and he was not at a loss for words.

Mr. Karst turned a charming smile on Susan and addressed her with polite gravity. "My dear Miss Susan, a pleasure to see you again. You are looking enchanting. I wonder if you would mind if I sought a word alone with your sister?"

"Not at all, Mr. Karst," Susan replied, dimpling. "Have you come on an important errand?" she asked pertly.

"Yes, indeed I have. But it is for your sister's ears alone," he answered solemnly.

Susan gave a magnificent sniff and stalked from the room. Kate, who had known all the other young gentlemen who called that day since childhood, had only met Mr. Karst the previous evening at the Assembly Rooms in Clifton. She surveyed him critically from his curly rust-colored locks to his polished boots. It was all very well for old friends to take part in this hoax, but she was not prepared for a stranger.

"May I offer you some refreshment, sir?" she asked coldly.

"Yes, if you please. I find myself in great need of a glass of wine."

Kate narrowed her eyes thoughtfully at his impudent tone as she summoned the butler. She refused to be goaded and proceeded to discuss the state of the weather in fatiguing detail. Mr. Karst watched her closely and admired her poise in the face of this fantastic onslaught of suitors. Her brown curls were arranged more casually than the previous evening, and worn under a wisp of lace which he presumed was meant for a cap. His study did not cause the large brown eyes to waver nor the arched brows to lift. She was attractive, if not beautiful, with a full mouth and high forehead, a straight, short nose, and a determined chin. There was an openness about her countenance which made him feel slightly uncomfortable in the present circumstances, but she sat at her ease, the trimness of her form enhanced by the jonquil gown.

When Sampson had with a snap set the silver tray bearing one glass and a bottle of fine Madeira on the side table, he unknowingly imitated Susan by giving a pronounced sniff before departing. Mr. Karst, at a sign from Kate, helped himself to a glass of wine and nonchalantly seated himself on a Chippendale chair close to the sofa.

"My dear Miss Montgomery," Karst began lazily, as he took a pinch of snuff from the little enamelled box, "I hope you will allow me to call you Kate."

"I think not, Mr. . . . Forgive me, I have forgotten your name."

"Karst, ma'am. Benjamin Karst." His snapping eyes betrayed his momentary annoyance, then he smiled with what he undoubtedly considered a most winning grace and continued, ''I fear I have been presumptuous. But I shall not be deterred. I know we have met only briefly and yet I am moved by your beauty, your wit, your superior understanding to declare myself.'' The tone of mockery was undaunted by the ''Harumph'' which issued from the object of his attentions. ''I would be the happiest of men were you to allow me to make you my wife.''

''Would you? How kind of you, Mr. . . . ah . . . Karst. And tell me, sir, what are your prospects?'' Kate asked softly.

''I assure you they are very good. I reached my majority two years ago and came into a most profitable estate but thirty miles from here. It includes an elegant manor house over which you would preside to perfection.'' Mr. Karst felt rather pleased with himself for this touch.

''I am intrigued. Where is this estate?''

''Not far from Yeovil, Miss Montgomery. Very pretty country it is there.''

''Indeed. And your family, Mr. Karst? Tell me of them. I must weigh the matter carefully, you know, as I am no longer in the first blush of youth. But then we appear to be of an age, so no doubt you will understand.''

There was no gainsaying that this gambit left Mr. Karst nonplussed, but Kate managed not to show her delight. Instead she puckered her face in a caricature of concentration and concern, as Mr. Karst's face paled visibly.

''I am three and twenty, Miss Montgomery, and—''

''I knew it!'' she declared triumphantly. ''We *are* of an age!''

"And my family, as I was saying, though it did not come over with the Conqueror, is a very ancient and respected one. My father purchased the late Marquess of Trentmere's estate ten miles from here several years ago, and my parents, my sister Selina, and I have resided there since."

"I thought you had arrived since I went to Daventry three years ago. And how do you find the neighborhood, Mr. Karst?" Kate was in charge of the situation now, and she watched the young man squirm as she pressed him for more and more details about himself, his family, and his position. It would obviously have been intolerably rude with a newly met acquaintance to have asked the half of the questions she now bombarded him with, but she had the protection of considering him a possible suitor. Not by a flicker of the eyes or a twitch of the lips did she betray her profound amusement at his discomfort. She could not have been so cruel to her old friends, though she could have wrung their necks cheerfully, but on this stranger who had lent himself to an apparently senseless hoax she could wreak her revenge. Finally, a little ashamed of herself, she put an end to the charade.

"Mr. Karst, you have been most patient and gratifyingly explicit in answer to my very personal questions. I now know more about you than you could possibly wish me to. I am sorry to have so discomfited you. Believe me, our conversation will go no further. I feel certain we should not suit, Mr. Karst, though I am conscious of the honor you do me in offering for me. Never do so again." She laughed, inviting him to share her joke.

Mr. Karst was not devoid of a sense of humor, fortunately, and promised with becoming sincerity not to broach the subject of marriage again. Kate rose and gave him her hand in parting, saying, "You may now call me Kate, it you wish."

"Nothing would give me more pleasure, Kate," he responded ruefully. "I was worried for a moment there."

"And you deserved to be. For I would tolerate this prank from my friends, Mr. Karst, but not from a stranger. I shall not quiz you on its source, for I gather you are bound to secrecy. But I shall get to the bottom of it."

"I have no doubt you shall, Kate, if this is a sample of your tactics. Try your brother. And do call me Benjamin. We deserve to be friends now, I hope."

"I hope so, too, Benjamin."

When he had left and Susan once again appeared, Kate was working at her embroidery frame, smiling to herself. "Why was he here so long, Kate? You surely did not accept him! You met him only last evening."

"No, goose. But it was very wrong of him to take part in this mischief, and so I let him know. I think there were no hard feelings."

"Do you look for more of them, Kate? Did you find out anything from him?"

"I didn't press him. They are obviously sworn to reveal nothing, but he did suggest that Ralph knows the whole story. Is he back yet?"

"No, and I have kept a watch for him. How could he be a party to such a prank against you, Kate? Your own brother!" Susan exclaimed with disgust.

"Ralph would only see the humor in it, you know, and would not have the sensibility to look beyond to the embarrassment for me. Ralph has never been particularly noted for his tact, I fear, unless he has developed some since I departed for Aunt Eleanor's,'' Kate rejoined wryly.

"Ramshackle fellow. He cannot know the meaning of the word, I'll be bound. I think perhaps there are no more, as Mr. Karst was here so long that another was sure to have shown up by now if there were. Did you do something outrageous at the Assembly that I did not see?"

"Not that I am aware of. How should I? It was pleasant to see everyone again, and I enjoyed myself enormously.''

"Well, it cannot be that they have just heard of your inheritance, for that has been general knowledge these three years past." Susan did not heed the frown of her sister's countenance, but continued blithely, "Though, to be sure, you have not been around to be offered for since you became such an heiress. Still, I do not see that that would have produced five eligible parties on one day for you. I am most distressed that Lord Norris was one of them, you know, Kate, for Mama and I had thought he was showing a decided preference for me.''

"And so he is. Don't be such a nodcock. It was only a game to him, as with the others, though God knows how poor Wayne got involved in it.''

"Lord Norris shall pay for this," Susan promised, with a flounce of her skirts and a twinkle in her eye.

"I cannot doubt it. But he can be no more than twenty, Susan, and he must still be a ward of the Earl of Winterton.''

"What does that matter? He is older than I am, and I think even the Earl could not find it an unsuitable match.''

"No, I suppose not, but the Earl is not particularly noted for his reasonableness, if I remember correctly.

However, this whole prank has convinced me that the young men hereabouts are by far too unoccupied with serious matters. I imagine it would be entertaining to do something about that,'' Kate mused thoughtfully.

''Oh, Lord, and you are but just come home,'' Susan sighed.

2

Ralph Montgomery spent the day in Bristol replenishing his already overflowing and dashing wardrobe. Even this activity did not consume the whole of the day, and he was having second thoughts about the propriety of the escapade unfolding at Montgomery Hall. It was not that he was concerned for his sister Kate's sensibilities, but that his father might catch wind of the affair and not see it in the proper light. His father, although generally a mild man, had quite a blistering tongue when he chose to use it. And he chose to use it not infrequently with his heir, despite that young man's advanced age of six and twenty.

Ralph found it expedient on this gray January day to while away the hours in Bristol for as long as he was able. When he had managed to lose a hundred pounds in a brandy-laced card game, the obliging winner offered to show him a horse which could be purchased quite reasonably by such a knowledgeable person as himself. Ralph prided himself on his judgment of horseflesh above all else and, in fact, when not in his cups, was quite an authority.

The two men made their way across the bustling inn yard to the stables where this reputedly magnificent beast was temporarily housed. Mr. Jeffreys sadly informed his young companion that due to his imminent trip abroad, he was forced to sell this favorite animal. The two discussed the bay's points in a friendly if bosky fashion and were dickering over price when they were interrupted by the Earl of Winterton, a rugged-featured man well-known to Ralph.

The Earl, in search of his groom, took one look at the bay and rapped out, "Showy. Too short in the back, Montgomery. Wouldn't touch him." Then he strode off with an arrogant shrug and without a backward glance.

Ralph flushed to the roots of his lank, blond hair, which he wore fashionably if unfortunately in the current *à la titus* style. His smoldering gaze followed the Earl until he was out of earshot and then he ripped up, "Top-lofty, self-consequential prig!" Ralph was not unaware, however, of the Earl's reputation as a non-pareil and a breeder of the finest horses in the area. So Mr. Jeffreys found himself dismissed rather curtly, and the disgruntled young Montgomery retired to the inn for his dinner, a good portion of which he drank. He was therefore a trifle foxed when he returned to Montgomery Hall and was not at all in the mood to be besieged by his two sisters seeking an account of the day's happenings. In point of fact, he had forgotten what had been happening at his home, lost as he was in his mortification at the Earl's criticism and his own gambling loss, which had cut well into his quarter's allowance.

Kate and Susan had waited impatiently through the evening, determined to have the truth from him. Their mother had spent the better part of the day in bed with the headache, and their father had been out inspecting a drainage system, so they had managed to keep the incident to themselves, much as Sampson was obviously bursting to spread the word. The butler was fond of Kate, however, and she had told him kindly but firmly that she would handle the matter herself. He had grunted disapprovingly and cast his eyes heavenward, but had indicated that he would respect her wishes.

Since Ralph did not arrive at his home until rather late, he found his sisters in his bedroom. "What the devil are you doing here?" he demanded.

"We want to know what has been happening today," Susan began, clutching at his coat sleeve.

"What I do is no affair of yours," Ralph retorted, shaking off her hand impatiently.

"I am sure we have not the slightest interest in what you did today," Kate commented appeasingly. "I wish for an explanation of the five offers of marriage I received during the course of the afternoon."

Enlightenment brought only sulky annoyance from her brother. "How should I know why you received five offers?" he rejoined.

"I am sure you know exactly why I received them. How could you involve yourself in a prank which would embarrass me so, Ralph?"

"Embarrass you? Why should they embarrass you, for God's sake? No more than a good joke," he said gloomily, his blurry eyes suddenly fixed on her.

"A rather shabby one, dear brother. Perhaps you had forgotten the consequences of the last offer I rejected in this neighborhood," his sister countered, her eyes forcing him to attend to her.

Ralph had thought his mortification for the day complete and that his head could not possibly hurt more than it already did, but he was wrong. He threw himself on his bed and groaned miserably. His eyes were shut, as he was unable to face his sister's penetrating look. Susan, a bit at a loss now, began to remove his dirty riding boots, glancing nervously at her sister from time to time.

"Rejected the lot of them, didn't you?" Ralph mumbled.

"Of course I did, chucklehead. But word of this day's work could spread throughout the area, and it can only cause me and the rest of the family discomfort. People are not likely to have forgotten about Carl so soon, in spite of the three years since his death. Oh, Ralph, how could you?"

"Wasn't my idea!" he blurted. "We went to an inn after the Assembly for some refreshment. The damn Rooms are always so hot and crowded, and there's not a thing worth drinking there. And it was early!" he exclaimed, as though this justified the whole plot.

"How did it come about, Ralph?" Kate asked calmly.

"Well, naturally, some of them began talking of you because you've been away so long. There was some talk of Carl's legacy, too," he moaned as he remembered, "but that was quickly set aside, as the Earl was there with a . . . companion. Not with us, you understand. Other side of the taproom. I doubt he heard us," he added unconvincingly. The six of them had not been particularly wary of their tongues under the influence of an excellent brandy. "Terence Marsh mentioned something you said. It's all your own fault," he complained.

Kate ignored this to ask, "What did I say to attract his attention? He seemed totally wrapped up in the Karst girl the entire evening. I am not even aware that I spoke to him."

"Perhaps not. He overheard you talking to Lady Romsey of your travels with Aunt Eleanor." Ralph massaged his temples carefully to soothe the aching before continuing. "Terence said you spoke of an event that took place in a country market. Something about a man bringing his wife to market with a rope about her neck and selling her to the highest bidder for five shillings."

"Yes, I remember telling Lady Romsey that. I believe she shared my horror at the scene."

"Well, Terence said you made some comment on the slavery of women. Then everyone began talking about how any woman your age would gladly accept marriage to anyone rather than remain single. Slavery or no. Most natural thing for a wager to come of it. Wayne Norris objected, but we overruled him. Drew lots to see who came first. Geoff lost. Went quite white, you know, as it would not seem singular to you when the first one offered."

"Certainly not. I have been away from home for three years, and it would not seem singular that a young man offer for me the day after my first social appearance," Kate scoffed. "Addlepate! Could you not have stopped it? You are, after all, my brother, my *elder* brother, though there are times I find it hard to believe!"

Stung, Ralph retorted, "I thought it would serve to bring you down a peg or two, my girl. All this travelling and independence are not for women. You have come to think yourself too good for the rest of us!"

Susan interrupted with, "That is not true, Ralph, and you know it. You are jealous of Kate for her adventures, that's all."

Kate stepped in to put an end to the bickering between her two siblings. "Never mind. I was unaware that I had been putting on airs about the house. I shall guard against it in future. Shall I call your man for you, Ralph?"

"Kate, I am truly sorry. Should have put a stop to it," he said contritely. "I'll make them keep it mum. Promise you. Send Walker to me, will you?"

When his sisters had left him to the ministrations of his valet, he vowed, not for the first time, to moderate his consumption of brandy. He did not seem to do his best reasoning when under the influence of the stuff. Sleep overcame him in a muddle of thoughts about his friend Carl, his sisters needing his protection, and the wager he had made for a race with Karst.

Susan accompanied her sister to Kate's room, as she refused to be dismissed until she had gotten to the source of this new mystery. "I remember Carl," she blurted, "but what did he have to do with all this?"

"Oh, Susan, you were too young at the time to be involved, but I suppose you had best know a bit now." Kate sighed. "Carl and Ralph were great friends, of course, so you probably saw Carl about the house. It was five years ago, and I was eighteen, as you are now. When Carl offered for me I refused him, for he was like another brother to me, and I could not think of him as a husband. There should have been no more to it than that. But Carl took it badly and said if he could not marry me he would join the forces in the Peninsula, which upset his mother greatly. The Countess was always a delicate woman and could not bear the thought of her youngest in the thick of war."

When Kate paused, her sister interjected, "I remember her, too. Such a beautiful woman, but so frail the year before she died."

"Yes. I was very fond of her. She tried to urge me to marry Carl, but I simply could not do it. She even sent the Earl to speak with me. He was very fond of his younger brother and in the ordinary course of things

would probably have considered me unworthy of Carl.
So it went against the grain with him to talk to me,
and I found him intolerably rude. You understand, Susan, that none of that should have happened. Mama
and Papa were very good; they did not press me. They
were flattered that I had been offered for by such a fine
young man of such good standing. But they respected
my wishes, especially Papa. I know he kept a rein on
Mama.''

Kate distractedly ran a shapely hand through her
brown curls, drawing them off her wide brow. Her
brown eyes were troubled and sad as she continued.
''Carl was seriously wounded in the Peninsula a year
or so later, and he died on the way home. His mother's
health declined after that, and she died a year later.
She came to see me before I went to stay with Aunt
Eleanor, and she was very kind to me. The Earl . . .
well, no matter. After Carl died . . . you see, I was
as fond of Carl as I am of Ralph, but I felt very uncomfortable here afterwards, and Aunt Eleanor asked
me to come and live with her. And there I have been
until she married again a month past.''

''But, Kate, how did it come that Carl left you
twenty thousand pounds?'' Susan asked. ''You were
not even betrothed to him.''

''It was his wish. I would have preferred not to accept it, but his brother forwarded a letter to me at Aunt
Eleanor's that had been found amongst his army belongings which had been separated from him. I could
not refuse his dying request, Susan.''

''Of course not,'' Susan replied loyally. ''But for
Ralph's stupidity it should all have been over long ago.
Now I have no doubt the whole story will be raked up
all over again, what with those muttonheads offering
for you in such a way, and you refusing them all.''

"I fear you are right, my love. But I am older now, and I shall manage, I assure you. And Ralph may be able to keep it quiet. Do not fret for me." Kate laughed, noting the frown on her sister's face.

"Yes, but you would like to marry, would you not? And now you have been made the butt of this joke, I cannot see who will marry you," Susan sighed, her eyes sparkling with tears of concern.

Kate hugged her sister and urged her off to bed, saying, "There is not a one in the lot of them I would consider, love. Perhaps I shall come to London with you, after all."

Susan did not manage to hide the distress this thought caused her in time to avoid Kate's sharp eyes. "I am only funning you, Susan," Kate quickly assured her, and smiled down at the bowed head of honey-blond hair. "I am far too old to share a London season with the likes of you, puss. Now run along. It's late."

3

Kate had the ability to sleep in almost any circumstance and consequently arose feeling rested, if restless. She was an early riser by nature and few of the household stirred as she swept out the massive front door and strode toward the stables for a ride before breakfast.

When she was galloping across the south pasturage she spied a rider on the bridle path leading from the village. He agitatedly motioned to her, and she reluctantly drew rein. It was Wayne Norris, once again looking flushed and unhappy.

"Wayne, I have heard the whole and I am surprised at you." She laughed as he joined her.

"Please say you will forgive me, Kate. I had no wish to participate but m' brother thought it safest if we both did, should our guardian catch wind of it."

"You are forgiven, Wayne, but how you should think he should not hear of it when he was present is beyond me," Kate replied with gentle mockery.

"Not precisely present, as you might say. He was rather occupied, you know. He takes very little interest in us unless it's to come the heavy over some escapade such as this."

"Well, I doubt you need fear he will do so this time.

I feel sure he will consider it quite an appropriate lesson for me.''

"You mustn't say so, Kate. No one holds you in anything but fond regard, and it is more than a pity that this particular episode should have occurred,'' Wayne protested urgently.

"Don't give it another thought. Are you up at Cambridge now?'' Kate asked, and proceeded to discuss his academic career as they rode along. Kate had spent most of the previous three years in a town boasting a Dissenter Academy and she was capable of maintaining a dialogue with Wayne on the nature of the studies offered and ignored. They parted genially, and it passed through Wayne's mind fleetingly that he would not be adverse to marrying such a woman as Kate Montgomery, jest or no jest. But he realized that she considered him a friend, and a very young one at that, since he was more of an age with her sister. Nonetheless, he rode off relieved that she had forgiven him.

Kate had no further encounters before she presented herself for breakfast. Her father and mother were at table, and Susan grinned conspiratorially at her. Ralph had not put in an appearance as yet, and Kate suspected that he would not for some hours to come.

Mr. Montgomery was genuinely pleased to have his daughter home; she was the only one who listened to his discourses on Thomas Coke's methods of farming with attention and pleasure. He was beginning to fear that Ralph would never take an interest in the property he would one day inherit. At six and twenty Ralph had no more serious thoughts in his head than he had had when he came down from Cambridge some years ago, which was to say, nothing beyond horses, hunting, and gambling. Fortunately, Mr. Montgomery's son was not always so unlucky at his gaming as he had been the previous day, but he was not always wise enough to know when he had encountered a Captain Sharp, either. Therefore, Mr. Montgomery, finding only one member of his family valued the knowledge he was acquiring and employing in farming, made no effort as some fathers might to stem Kate's sometimes unfeminine enthusiasms.

Mrs. Montgomery was quite as pleased as her husband to have Kate home; for although Susan was perhaps her favorite, being the baby of the family, the older woman was fond of her first daughter and relied on her to run the household more capably than she herself. Things went on so much more smoothly when Kate was home, her mother thought, smiling over her toast and tea. Such a dear girl. Though not so young anymore, she realized, and a frown ruffled her brow.

"Is something the matter, Mama?" Kate asked.

"No, dear. I was just thinking that you are getting on in years now, and we should be looking out for a husband for you."

Susan was shaken by a fit of giggles at this, and Kate threw her a warning glance. "You fear I shall be forever on your hands, dear Mama?" Kate quizzed her.

"I'm sure you are a great comfort to me, my love, but there is nothing like an establishment of your own. It is a woman's duty to marry and have a family."

"Her duty to whom?" Kate asked quietly before taking another sip of chocolate.

"Why, to herself, I suppose. Or to . . . well, to fit in with everyone else, you know," her mother fumbled.

"As to that, I cannot imagine that anyone else cares a fig whether I marry or not. And for myself, yes, I should like to marry, but not just to be married. I wish you could have seen Aunt Eleanor and Mr. Hall,

Mama, for they are so very well-suited and so fond of one another.''

"No doubt, my love, though why Eleanor should wish to remarry at her age is more than I can understand. Sir John left her well provided for. It must be quite uncomfortable to have to learn all those little things she must do and not do to make her new husband happy.''

"I cannot think she will mind, dear Mama. Mr. Hall has the most accommodating nature, and I'm sure they will rub on very well together.''

Mr. Montgomery glanced up from the paper to comment, "I, for one, wish them happy. You say they are to visit us on their return from their trip abroad, Kate?''

"It's their intention, though it will be several months, I imagine.''

The conversation, thus successfully diverted from the subject of marrying Kate off, dwindled to a companionable silence. Susan nudged her sister and grinned. "Shall we walk to the village this morning, Kate?'' she asked. "I am in need of some trimming for one of my bonnets.''

They set out on this expedition shortly after. Kate told her sister of her meeting with Wayne Norris that morning, and Susan wanted to know whether his brother had been with him.

"No. I think Wayne was coming to apologize, and I doubt that Charles will do so.''

"If Wayne was so against the scheme, he should not have partaken in it,'' Susan remarked scornfully.

"It appears his brother wanted moral support should their guardian learn of it. Are you still angry with Charles?''

"I am. He shall learn that he cannot play with my affections," Susan sniffed.

"I should shake were I in his boots," Kate allowed. "Speak of the devil!"

Striding down the muddy street toward them was Lord Norris himself, making a most determined effort to appear casual and at ease. This was belied, however, by the determined set of his smile and the quirk in his eyebrows. "Kate, Susan, a pleasure to meet you this morning. May I accompany you to your destination?"

Kate greeted him kindly, but Susan lowered her eyes and refused to speak to him. "I told you she would be annoyed, Charles," she whispered as she placed her hand on his arm. Susan would have looked awkward if she had trailed behind them, so she stiffly laid her hand on his other arm and paced reluctantly down the street with them. Kate maintained a conversation with Lord Norris, but her sister refused to respond to his repeated attempts to draw her out.

In exasperation he finally turned to her and blurted, "It was only a joke, Susan, and your sister has obviously accepted it as such. Why can't you?"

"You have not apologized to my sister for your senseless and tasteless joke, sir!" Susan cried.

Lord Norris was at a stand. He did not wish to apologize, for it would indicate he had been in the wrong, which he well knew. If he did not apologize, his enchanting Susan seemed quite capable of cutting him for good. As he hesitated, Susan became indignant and dashed across the street toward a shop on the other side, directly in the path of an oncoming curricle!

Lord Norris stood frozen, and Kate, who had stepped away from them to avoid their personal quarrel, swung back at his cry. As she dashed forward she was ruthlessly thrust aside, and her sister was swept out of the way of the now-plunging horses by the Earl of Winterton, who had emerged from a shop behind Kate. He carried Susan to the side of the road and exclaimed, "Now she's going to faint, drat the girl. Miss Montgomery, see to your sister!" His command was not necessary, but it roared over the considerable commotion in the street, nonetheless. Kate hastened to her sister's side and began chafing her wrists, while the Earl attempted to quiet the horses still plunging wildly. He addressed himself to Lord Norris, his ward, in no uncertain terms.

"Help me with these beasts, you slow-top! Think this is a party?"

Lord Norris at last sprang into action, and the horses were quickly settled. A shaken Benjamin Karst kept muttering, "She ran right in front of me!" He gave the reins to his groom so that he could descend from his bright scarlet curricle, but he had some difficulty in walking over to Kate and Susan, for his legs were trembling. "Is she all right, Kate?"

"I think so, Benjamin. She has merely fainted and is coming round now. Do not be alarmed."

"It's *my* fault," Lord Norris proclaimed dramatically, coming over to them. "I *do* apologize, Kate."

"Oh, do be still. I do not wish to hear another word on the subject, do you hear me? I have lost patience with the lot of you," Kate cried, her nerves strained intolerably.

"A most unhandsome acceptance of an apology," the Earl commented sarcastically.

Kate chose to ignore this remark. "Charles, will you help me get Susan to the inn? She should have a glass of wine."

"I'll get us a private parlor," Benjamin offered, and

was followed more slowly by Kate and Charles assisting Susan. When it became evident that the Earl intended to join them, Kate turned to him and dropped an exaggerated curtsy. "I must thank you for saving Susan's life, Lord Winterton. We would not wish to disturb you further."

"I'll leave when I'm ready, Miss Montgomery. Thompson, brandy for the lot of us, if you please," he directed the landlord.

"It is not necessary . . ." Kate began.

"I'll decide what's necessary, Miss Montgomery. You and Charles and Karst do not seem to have managed things so very well."

"But it wasn't my fault," Benjamin protested. "She ran right in front of me." Charles could think of nothing to say, and Kate merely glared at the Earl.

Susan whispered, "I am sorry to have given so much trouble. Thank you, Lord Winterton. I was most foolish, I know."

"Hush, my dear," her sister comforted her. "Sip this, and you will feel better," she urged, taking the glass the Earl handed her. When Susan had taken several sips, the color began to return to her face.

Kate was offered a glass by the Earl and shook her head. "Drink it," he ordered. "You need it."

Since this was no more than the truth, Kate acquiesced and savored the stinging warmth it evoked. She ignored the disdainful look the Earl bent on her.

"Do you think you can manage to get the two of them home safely, Karst?" Lord Winterton asked.

"*I* can see them home," Charles declared.

"Don't you think, Charles, that they would do better in Mr. Karst's curricle, even if they will be a bit crowded?" his guardian asked, his patience wearing thin.

"Yes, sir, I suppose so."

"Then give Karst a chance to answer for himself."

Benjamin did not like the Earl's tone, but he was more than willing to take the sisters to Montgomery Hall. "I can see them home safely," he muttered. "The accident was not my fault."

"Lord Winterton is not noted for his reasonableness in placing blame," Kate offered. "Do not be offended, Benjamin. We welcome your assistance." She helped her sister to her feet, and the three of them left. The door closed before they could hear more than "Stay, Charles. I have something to say to you" in the Earl's icy voice.

"I'd give much to hear that," Benjamin whispered to Kate.

"So should I," she replied, her eyes twinkling. "Poor Charles. He absolutely froze."

"I cannot say I did so well myself. You would have been under the horses' hooves as well, Kate, had he not thrust you aside."

"Tut! He has no patience with anyone. There was a time . . . but that was long ago," she faltered, remembering the Earl's kindness to Carl and his mother. "He has grown selfish and bitter, I fear."

"But he saved my life," Susan remarked rather forcefully. "I am grateful to him."

"So are we all. I am chastened; I should not have spoken so of him when he risked his life for you, my love. Forgive me."

"I did not mean to scold you, Kate. But you are always so fair. I have seldom heard you speak unkindly of anyone. Except in anger, of course," Susan remarked. "When you are angry or upset you do have a sharp tongue."

"How right you are! No one has ever accused me of having a placid temper," Kate agreed.

When they arrived at the Hall, Susan was immediately hustled up to her room, after once again apologizing to Benjamin for having frightened him by her carelessness. When she was advised of the circumstances of their arrival home, Mrs. Montgomery fluttered around her youngest chick. She scolded and petted in turn, until Kate was driven to distraction. But Susan obviously found this the necessary prescription, so Kate excused herself and went to the music room. She had managed to calm herself by playing a few airs on the pianoforte when Sampson intruded to announce Lord Norris.

"Is Mama still with Susan?" she asked.

"I believe so, Miss Kate."

"Then show him into the parlor. I shall join him in a minute."

Lord Norris sported the aggressive air of one who has just been severely and justly chastised and is unwilling to admit the right of it. He stomped about the room after greeting Kate darkly, finally stopping to speak.

"I have already apologized to you for yesterday. My guardian has informed me," he continued sarcastically, "that I chose an inappropriate moment and that I should express my regret again."

"Then perhaps your guardian did not hear me say that I do not wish to hear another word on the subject, apologies included," Kate flashed.

"I doubt that he cares what you want," Charles replied, "but I for one agree with you. Nevertheless, I am sorry if I caused you any embarrassment, Kate," he said contritely. "I have promised Winterton I will not speak of it, and of course Wayne will not. There now, that is over. Is Susan all right?''

"Mama is with her, but she seems well enough. I shall tell her you called, Charles.'' When the young man appeared reluctant to leave, Kate patted the seat beside her and suggested, "Sit down and tell me what is bothering you. Not the tongue-lashing from Winterton, surely?''

Charles could not seem to decide what tack to follow—indignation at his guardian for berating him or mortification at his own showing in the near-accident. Kate smiled encouragingly at him, and his self-doubts won out. "I feel such a fool, Kate!'' he exclaimed, agitatedly twisting the signet ring on his finger. "What must Susan think of me, standing there like an idiot while she was nearly trampled to death! And to have *him* be the one to save her. Even *you* were able to react faster than I, for I saw him fling you out of the way when you went after her. I shall die of shame!'' He could not keep the dramatic note from his voice, even though his feelings were real.

"Charles, you must not reproach yourself too severely, nor give in to self-pity. You are prone, I think, to do both. No one has any reason to doubt your courage. I can myself remember some rather daring episodes from your youth,'' she admitted with a laugh. "I think the shock overpowered your natural instinct. I feel sure Susan will understand, if you do not exaggerate the incident. But Susan is young and needs someone mature to lean on. I don't think yesterday's childish prank set you very high in her esteem, Charles.''

"No, I suppose not,'' he admitted grudgingly. "You don't think she needs someone really *old*, do you?''

"Not old, Charles. Mature. Someone she can depend on. Someone stable." Kate sighed. "I should hate to think of her marrying some loose-screw; she deserves better."

Charles eyed her suspiciously but decided that she could not possibly be referring to himself. He thanked her for her kindness and departed, leaving Kate to mull over the morning's adventures.

4

Susan was able to join the family for a luncheon set
back an hour by Kate, as Mrs. Montgomery had been
too occupied to remember. Ralph looked better than
Kate had expected, but he was given to morose
thoughts. It touched him on the raw to hear that the
Earl of Winterton had saved his youngest sister's life
while he lay abed nursing a splitting head. Mrs. Montgomery urged her husband to carry a letter to Winter
Manor and express their thanks to Winterton. He suggested that Ralph accompany him but was informed
that his son had other plans for the afternoon.

"And you, Kate? Should you like to ride with me?"
he asked.

"I would like to, Papa, but Mama is expecting call-
ers and I shall sit with Susan," Kate begged off.

Thus Mr. Montgomery set off alone carrying his
wife's letter to the Earl. His reception was no better
than he had expected; the Earl was not pleased to see
him, but he was ushered into the library and offered a
glass of wine after his ride.

"My daughters have apprised me of the great service you have done my family, Lord Winterton. I
wished to thank you personally," Mr. Montgomery
began.

"There is no need. I could not help but involve myself," Winterton responded. "Your younger daughter was a fool, and your elder daughter has an unruly tongue, sir. You should keep them on leads."

Mr. Montgomery could have taken offense at this unkind comment, but surprisingly he broke into a laugh. "You are too severe," he chuckled at last. "Tell me your opinion of my son."

"I stopped him only yesterday from buying a short-backed nag," Winterton retorted, but he grinned at Mr. Montgomery. "It cannot be pleasant to be the parent of such a bunch of chuckle-heads."

"They are well enough," Mr. Montgomery replied. "Not precisely what I had expected, to be sure, but not so bad, either. Your own father might not be over-impressed with such a stiff-rumped, arrogant son as yourself."

Winterton eyed him closely before saying, "I would not allow anyone else to say so to me, sir. My father was inordinately fond of you."

"And I of him. You're making a name for yourself in the neighborhood, Winterton, and it is not alto-gether flattering. Tell me, have you kept up his farming methods? Do you keep abreast of the Hookham Meetings?"

The two men spent an agreeable afternoon going over Lord Winterton's estate and discussing the various improvements accomplished and contemplated. If the neighbors found Winterton disagreeable, his tenants did not. Mr. Montgomery explained his own improvised method of drainage, and Winterton admitted he would like to see it. The two men parted amicably.

It was a week before Winterton availed himself of Mr. Montgomery's invitation to inspect the farming methods used at the Hall. Unfortunately he arrived on a day when Mr. Montgomery had gone to Bristol. Mrs.

Montgomery sought out Kate in the music room and begged her to take Lord Winterton about the estate in her father's stead.

"For you know almost as much about it as your father, Kate, and Ralph doesn't know a seed drill from a . . . a . . ."

"Winnowing fan. Yes, Mama, I know. But I am sure Lord Winterton would do better to come back another day when Papa is here to escort him himself."

"You are forgetting the obligation we are under to his lordship, Kate. He saved your sister's life, and I would not wish to show him any discourtesy."

"But he would probably be insulted if I took him around the estate," Kate protested. "Women are not supposed to know of such things."

"He seemed intrigued by the idea," her mother admitted.

"Ah, yes, I can imagine that sardonic look," Kate laughed. "All right, I'll do it. Tell him I shall be with him in ten minutes. I must change."

Kate was determined to wipe the sneer off Winterton's face, and she succeeded within the hour. She discussed the farming methods in such a businesslike, knowledgeable way that Winterton was unable to hide his fascination.

"It has taken me a few weeks to catch up," she confessed. "My Aunt Eleanor lives in town and I have been out of touch with the farming except through my father's letters. I saved all of those, though, and studied them so that I would not disappoint him on my return."

"Your father wrote you of such things?"

"Oh, yes, he writes more of crop rotation and drainage than of the family's activities. It is no surprise to me to hear how much hazel is sold for sheep

hurdles and chestnut for hop poles.'' She offered him
a mischievous grin. ''The only thing that surprises me
is that he does not have his writing paper stamped with
the Coke motto: No fodder, no beasts; no beasts, no
manure; no manure, no crop.''

Winterton grudgingly returned her smile. ''I could
tell he was an enthusiast when I spoke to him. Surely
he does not expect you to understand the farm imple-
ments and new sowing and harvesting methods.''

''Not only does he expect it, he insists on it. You
must not think I am adverse to learning, Lord Winterton. Why, *The Farmer's Magazine* is well-nigh my favorite reading.'' Her eyes danced, but her expression
remained politely blank.

''You are mocking, Miss Montgomery. No doubt
your interest does not extend to the financial side of
the estate management, which would be too compli-
cated for a woman.'' He was well aware that he was
purposely pinching at her, but he could not resist the
impulse to set her down, since his opinion had long
been that she was capricious and unprincipled. Had
she not refused to marry his brother Carl and then
accepted a large legacy from him?

Kate did not allow his disparaging comments to ir-
ritate her. ''The other knowledge would serve little
purpose if I were not also trained in keeping the books.
I have in the past taken over when my father was ill or
away from home. He does not believe in teaching the
practice without the theory, my lord, or having me
aware of the income without knowing the expenses. I
am rather fond of doing the accounts.''

''Are you? You astonish me, Miss Montgomery. I
have prided myself no less than your father on keeping
abreast of agricultural matters, and I am impressed by

the extent of your knowledge. Does your brother take a like interest?''

"Unfortunately, no, but I have an eye to that," Kate remarked with a casual wave of her hand. "Has Lord Norris shown any interest in his estate?"

"Strange you should ask that. The young gudgeon came to me but a few days ago—I'll be bound it's the first time he has ever sought me out—and asked how he should go about learning something of estate management. I thought he was roasting me for a moment, but he was dead serious."

"Then there is hope for Ralph yet, I feel sure."

Winterton eyed her suspiciously and asked, "Did you have something to do with Charles's sudden interest in his estate?"

"Now, how should I, Lord Winterton? I imagine it was the peal you rang over him."

"He told you of that? Young jackanapes. Forever acting tragedies."

"You are too hard on him. He is young yet," Kate replied coolly.

"At his age I came into my inheritance," Winterton retorted.

"And I am sure your handling of it was above reproach," she replied sweetly.

"I didn't know a thing about it," he admitted, "but there were people who depended on me."

"Charles does not have the same motivation, perhaps."

"No, for I am convinced his brother Wayne shows all the earmarks of a scholar."

"Does that bother you?" Kate asked, directing her mare back toward the stables.

"No, the life will suit him. He's not a bad fellow,

Wayne. I'm surprised he took part in that prank last week.''

"He didn't wish to, you know. He came to me first thing the next morning to apologize. You should not have sent Charles. He was in pelter enough, and you could not but have heard me say I did not wish to speak of it again," she said tartly, remembering her annoyance. "It had nothing to do with you."

"My wards do as I tell them, Miss Montgomery," he replied stiffly. "I am responsible for their behavior as gentlemen."

Kate burst out laughing at this. "When you set them such a fine example, I am surprised you need speak to them at all."

"I told your father you had an unruly tongue. It is most unbecoming."

"No, do you think so? Tsk. I must mend my ways for such an authority!" she exclaimed and set her mare to the gallop. Despite his later start, Winterton managed to arrive at the stables before she did and glared as he handed her down. "I have enjoyed the opportunity to show you about the estate, Lord Winterton."

"Thank you for your time, Miss Montgomery," he replied formally before he remounted his horse, lifted his hat to her, and rode off. She watched him out of sight, his tall frame erectly at ease in the saddle. His rugged countenance was accentuated by the penetrating blue eyes and black hair, and his athletic build suggested a forceful masculinity. If his eyebrows were not so fierce and his nose not so determinedly patrician, he might be considered handsome, she supposed, but with such an unbending, unconciliating manner, he virtually denied one the right to pass upon his features.

* * *

Kate joined her sister, who was reading the latest novel from the circulating library in the parlor. Susan looked up and grinned at her sister. "Mama said you had taken Lord Winterton about the estate. Was it fun?"

"Well, for a while he was pleasant, but I managed to annoy him in the end. He told me that I have an unruly tongue and that it is most unbecoming," Kate confessed with mock contrition. "Are we expecting Benjamin Karst this afternoon? He seems a frequent caller these days. I fear you have bewitched another eligible man."

"Nonsense. He pays no more attention to me than to you, as you well know, and I think he would just as soon find Ralph as either of us, for they have some lark planned, I think."

"The word is about in the stables they are planning some crackbrained race to Bath at night. Hmm. I think, Susan, it's time we gave their thoughts a different direction."

Susan groaned. "What now, my dear?"

"They share a common interest in horses, and I know just the farm where they could breed them."

"What do they know about breeding horses? They'd make wretched work of it. Besides, Papa would not be willing to advance the funds for such a scheme."

"You may be right, love, but shan't we at least give it a try?" Kate begged. "We would all be more comfortable if we could find something to interest Ralph besides gaming and hunting."

"Oh, very well. Tell me what I am to do."

When Benjamin put in an appearance that afternoon, it was not difficult to arrange that Ralph join the three of them for a ride. With a grin to Kate, Susan declared, "Benjamin, you must have a fine eye for a horse. I have never seen such a marvelous animal."

Cutting short Benjamin's gracious acceptance of this compliment, Kate said with enthusiasm, "You should have seen the horse Lord Winterton was riding today, Susan. It is no wonder he has such a reputation for breeding them. I've seldom seen such a magnificent animal."

"Oh, he's good enough, I suppose," Ralph interjected, still smarting under his lordship's recent criticism. "But I have no doubt Benjamin or I could do as well if we had the opportunity."

"Come now. You and Benjamin both have a good eye, I feel sure, but there is more to breeding excellent horses than that. What do you know of their care and the proper combinations to produce a prime goer?" Kate teased.

"As much as the next one," Benjamin retorted.

"Not as much as Lord Winterton," Susan chimed in.

"Well, he has been doing it for some years. Probably reads the journals, too. And he has good land for them," Benjamin added.

"Then you couldn't do it," Kate mused, "for you haven't been at it for years, and I am sure you would not touch a journal, though of course there is good land to be had."

"Where?" the two young men asked in chorus.

"Mr. Drew's farm, for example. I have heard he has put it up for sale. Since it touches on Lord Winterton's lands, I imagine it must be quite as suitable for pasturing horses. I wonder if Papa would be interested? But then, Lord Winterton will probably snap it up. The Carruthers farm is available, too, for with the end of the war and the drop in corn prices they are feeling the pinch and plan to go to Ireland, I'm told.''

"What say we ride over and look out the Drew farm?'' Benjamin asked. "It's not far.''

"I've no objection,'' Susan agreed with a sparkling glance cast at Kate.

Ralph merely grunted, "Would be just like Winterton to snatch up some good land before anyone else has a chance to see it.''

The farm was a pleasant, well-maintained one of good size. Mr. Drew had no objection to their riding about it. It was necessary for Kate to comment on the farming methods used, the crops likely to be raised there, the lack of adequate drainage, and the improvements which could be made to produce a better yield. Ralph and Benjamin showed a moderate interest in her disclosures, but were more concerned with the pasturage and inadequate stables. Kate did not wish to press the point and dropped back to ride with Susan.

"At least you have them interested, though I think they would make a horrid failure of it, Kate,'' Susan remarked. "They know nothing.''

"No. It's excellent land, though, and Papa would be a guiding hand. We shall just have to see if anything comes of it. I must have a word with Papa.''

It was several hours before Kate was able to speak with her father. She found him in his study, where he welcomed her and thanked her for showing Winterton about the estate.

"Is he still convinced that my three offspring are chuckle-heads?'' he asked her, his face serious but his eyes laughing.

"I assure you, sir, he was impressed with my knowledge, but not with my unruly tongue,'' Kate offered.

"You have set his back up again, child? Why must you always do that?"

"He has been hard on me for no good reason, Papa, and I cannot like his high and mighty air. He is forever dictating to someone."

"Would you like him better if people took advantage of him?"

"Of course not. But there must be some middle ground, some softness of heart."

"He was very devoted to his brother and to his mother, Kate. You cannot have forgotten that," he said sadly.

"No, you are right, Papa. I shall try to mind my manners in future," Kate said penitently. "It was not about him I came to speak, but of Ralph."

"Meddling again, my dear?"

"You might call it that. He may, if all goes well, approach you with a scheme for purchasing the Drew farm."

"Whatever would interest him in such a thing?"

"He and Benjamin Karst have recently developed a desire to breed horses, you know."

"I didn't know. You put a flea in their ears?"

"Yes, for it seems to me the best way to get Ralph interested in the land is for him to have something to do with it. He *is* a good judge of horses when he keeps his mind on business. If he and Benjamin were to start an endeavor, you would be in a position to lead them through it successfully," Kate pointed out.

"It could be a condition of a loan that he farm the property profitably while he is getting into the breeding of horses," Mr. Montgomery said thoughtfully. "Is the Drew acreage worth the endeavor?"

"I doubt it shows much of a profit now, for though it is well-maintained, I cannot see that the latest developments are being employed. There is definitely potential there. If Ralph does not wish it . . . well, never mind. I hope he will come to you. He does not realize Susan and I plotted his downfall from the gentleman of leisure, you understand.''

''Susan has taken to meddling, too, now?'' her father sighed.

''Susan must needs learn that the inequities of the law with regard to women can only be equalized by the use of a little strategy where men are concerned,'' Kate protested. ''It will do her no harm, for there is no malice in her.''

''You spent too long in Daventry, Kate.''

5

A week later there was a heavy snow and a great freeze. The Hall park was mounded with drifts, the trees covered with the white lace and hanging icicles of the season. Kate had been excluded from any discussions on the Drew farm, if there had been any. She knew her father had ridden over to see it some days before, but he was close-mouthed with Kate.

"I have no doubt he is annoyed with me for interfering," Kate told Susan, as they were enjoying tea that afternoon. "He likes my knowing about the estate, but he takes exception to my meddling, as he calls it."

"If he is miffed, he will soon get over it. You know he cannot be displeased with you for long."

"So I hope."

They were interrupted by Sampson bearing a letter on a silver platter which he offered to Kate. When he had left, Kate broke the seal and exclaimed, "It's from Charity! You won't mind if I read it now, will you, Susan?" After a moment she continued, "She's in Bath with her mother and sister. Famous! I shall ask Mama right away if I may have her to visit for a spell. She is the most delightful person, Susan, and quite beautiful."

"We should have a party while she is here," Susan contributed helpfully.

"With this weather, it should be a skating party," Kate replied.

"We have not done that for years! Let's. I love gliding around with a huge muff and sitting by the fire drinking steaming chocolate. Do you suppose we could?"

"I see no reason not to, if Mama is agreeable. I shall speak with her."

Within the hour Kate had dispatched a letter to her friend offering to meet the coach from Bath five days hence in Bristol at noon. The skating party became an established plan, and invitations were sent out to most of the young people in the neighborhood, including four of Kate's erstwhile suitors, as Wayne had returned to Cambridge.

"That's one nice thing about a skating party," Susan giggled, as she dipped her pen in the standish. "There are so few of our elders around to spoil the fun."

"And there are no limits to the time you spend with one person as there are at a ball, Susan. Whom do you plan to spend so much time with, puss?" Kate quizzed her.

"It is just that I have seen so little of Charles these days. He seems to be taking an unusual interest in his estate of a sudden. Kate, did you meddle there, too?" Susan asked indignantly.

"Well, I do not wish to see you become attached to some flibbertigibbet. I merely told him that you needed someone mature and stable."

"You mean he's doing this for me?" Susan asked, flattered. "You really are a corker, Kate."

"I plan to take a break from my endeavors for a

while now,'' Kate laughed, ''and enjoy Charity's
visit.''

Kate chose to meet her friend herself a few days
later, so she took the cabriolet with the groom up behind. Driving was one of her favorite activities, but
she had no wish to have a pair in hand on a day which
threatened more snow. She piled a fur-lined rug about
her and left in good time, keeping a close watch on
the sky. The stagecoach was on time, and Charity
Martin-Smith stepped down eagerly to greet her friend.

''I am so pleased you could come,'' Kate cried.

''And I. You would not believe the average age of
the community in Bath, my dear. My mother is a com-
parative youngster!'' Charity laughed.

''I have not had the pleasure of being there for years,
but I shall take your word for it. Come, Harris will
see to your luggage. It's bitterly cold, but we have the
coziest rug, and the Hall is not so very far.''

Kate kept the horse at a sedate pace as they negoti-
ated the muddy roads of Bristol and turned onto the
frozen lanes beyond. Charity had much to tell her
friend about acquaintances from Daventry, and Kate
attended her as best she could, but the snow had begun
to fall suddenly and heavily, making visibility poor.
Kate could hear horses approaching from the opposite
direction and clung to the side of the road. But the
oncoming vehicle was not sharing her caution, and
coming around a bend she found it directly before her
in the middle of the lane. Upon sighting her, the driver
instantly and skillfully reined his horses away, but he
was not in time. Kate had brought the cabriolet to a
halt, but it was struck by the curricle's wheel and
tipped over against the bank.

Charity and Kate were jostled but found themselves
unharmed. Harris ran to the horse to calm him, and

the other driver righted the carriage swiftly. Kate took one look at the driver of the curricle and muttered, "If he's not saving us from accidents, he's causing them!"

Winterton had been approaching her at the time and overheard this plaintive cry. "Are you and your companion all right, Miss Montgomery?"

"Yes, thank you, Lord Winterton." She was strongly tempted to add "No thanks to you" but remembered her father's words and refrained.

"There appears to be no damage to the horse or carriage other than a scratch. Of course I shall . . ."

"Good God, Andrew, what's keeping you? I am like to freeze to death before we reach Bristol," a pettish voice interjected, growing louder as its owner neared them.

"You would be warmer in the curricle, Celeste," Winterton commented dryly, noting her snow-covered slippers and the damp hem of her bizarre purple pelisse.

Nothing drew Kate's attention, however, so much as the amazing confection on the woman's head, which appeared to consist entirely of bright pink ostrich plumes which waved in the cold breeze and tickled against the small, delicately featured face. Since the face was also rouged and painted, Kate had no trouble in recognizing her as a Cyprian, and Kate's eyes began to dance. She said kindly, "Do not let us keep you, Lord Winterton. There is no damage to speak of, and you must be as chilled as your companion. We're off, Harris," she called to the groom, who resumed his position. She drew away from the glowering Winterton and flicked the whip in a gesture of farewell.

"Who was that?" Charity queried. "He seemed very annoyed with you, and he was totally at fault."

"He knows it, and that is why he was annoyed. To say nothing of his companion. Was she not priceless, Charity?"

"Very fancy," Charity agreed solemnly.

"I think I have told you of Lord Winterton. Carl was his brother," Kate explained.

"You have. He is still bullying you?"

"Yes. He considers me beneath contempt for accepting the inheritance from Carl when I had refused to marry him."

"You should explain the circumstances to him, my love."

"There is no need. What can it matter how he thinks of me?" her friend replied stubbornly.

"That's your pride talking, Kate."

"I know it," she sighed. "But I see no reason to seek to explain my actions to a man who has already judged me unworthy."

"You must decide for yourself; I am sure you will do what is right."

"Your faith in me is flattering, Charity. I hope I may deserve it."

"Papa says having faith in people gives them the strength to be their best."

"I miss your father," Kate admitted. "Here is the Hall. I shall let Harris take the carriage to the stables. And, Harris, not a word of the accident, please."

All of the Montgomerys were there to meet them. Kate made no mention of their mishap, and Charity followed her lead. They accepted the tea gratefully and sat close to the blazing hearth. Charity made an instant captive of Ralph, who could scarcely believe the vision who had just walked into the Hall was real. She was a tall girl with reddish-gold hair, an oval face, and a stately carriage. Her frock was of emerald green muslin, not in the height of fashion, but extremely becoming to her, with a high lace collar framing her face and flowing lace at her wrists. Susan had a fleeting moment of jealousy as she surveyed her sister's friend, but she soon lost it as her admiration of Charity grew. There was a calmness and dignity about Miss Martin-Smith which could not be ignored.

Susan explained that they were having a skating party in a few days' time, and Charity joined in her enthusiasm. She was also ready to hear all about Susan's plans for her London season. But she admitted to Kate later when they were alone in Charity's room that the thought of such an exhausting whirl at her age quite overcame her.

"You are no older than I," Kate pointed out, "but I should not like it, either. Mama did not insist that I have a season when I was Susan's age, and after that . . . well, there was no question of it. A Marriage Mart is very little more than an auction to the highest bidder. Thank Heaven my parents would not push Susan into a marriage she did not wish. It should do her good to see some new faces, though she may end up with Lord Norris in the end. I must tell you of the prank these young rascals played a few weeks ago."

Charity was upset for her friend over these revelations and relieved that Ralph had succeeded in silencing the affair. She was amused at Kate's attempts to find the young men more ambitious projects. In fact, she felt quite in the picture of the neighborhood by the next afternoon when she and Kate and Mrs. Montgomery were sitting chatting in the parlor. Sampson arrived to announce Lord Winterton, and the young women exchanged a mischievous glance.

Mrs. Montgomery was startled at this social call and a bit put out by the grim look on Winterton's face.

He bowed to her politely and exchanged a few pleasantries before turning to the young women.

He addressed Kate when he said, "I have come to assure myself that—"

Kate gave a warning shake of her head and interrupted, "Lord Winterton, I do not believe you have met my friend from Daventry, Miss Martin-Smith. Charity, this is Lord Winterton, a neighbor of ours."

Conversation was kept to local matters and the state of the weather for some time, and Kate was amused by Winterton's growing restlessness. Mrs. Montgomery was finally given a sign by her daughter and gladly excused herself.

"As I started to say before, Miss Montgomery," Winterton declared, "I came to assure myself of your well-being after the accident, and to apologize for it. You did not give me a chance to do so yesterday. Did you not tell your parents?"

"No, I saw no reason to alarm them, for there was little harm done. You are a hero to them for saving Susan's life, and it seemed a pity to blemish your record," Kate replied.

"Perhaps Kate has suffered a stiff neck from the accident," Charity suggested, the mild censure alleviated by a twinkle in her eye.

"Miss Montgomery always has a stiff neck," Winterton retorted.

"Enough. I appreciate your calling, Lord Winterton, but as you see, we are perfectly recovered from the mishap. I hope you and your companion are likewise," Kate could not resist adding.

It was the first time she had seen him smile, and the change in his countenance was remarkable. The forbidding black eyebrows over the penetrating blue eyes relaxed, and his grimly set lips twitched into a twisted

grin. "You are an admirable opponent, Miss Montgomery. I suffered no more than a knock to my pride,
and my companion, though she may never drive with
me again, suffered no more than wet feet."

"I am pleased to hear it," Kate responded with a
smile to match his.

If Lord Winterton had taken his leave at this point,
Kate would probably have retained an improved im-
pression of him. Unfortunately, he recalled at that moment a grievance which was on his mind, and the black
brows and wide mouth returned to their former stern-
ness.

"I believe your brother and Benjamin Karst are
negotiating to purchase the Drew farm," he began.

"Are they? That is good news indeed," Kate replied.

"You would have me believe you knew nothing of
it?" Winterton asked sarcastically.

"I do not care what you believe," Kate flashed.

"I'm sure Lord Winterton would understand if you
explained to him, Kate," Charity suggested helpfully.

"He understands only what he wishes to," Kate retorted and walked stiffly from the room.

"There are few who could rival her for temper,"
Winterton remarked succinctly, rising to leave.

"There are few who rouse her to it as you do, I'll
be bound," Charity replied. "I have known Kate for
years and seen her lose her temper only once before."

"But she did know of her brother's plans, Miss
Martin-Smith, for he told me himself, quite triumphantly I might add, that she had ridden over the property with him."

"Kate may have given her brother the idea, Lord
Winterton, but she has not been kept abreast of its
progress by her family. I'm sure you will wish me to

convey your apologies to her," Charity added serenely.

Winterton eyed her malevolently for a moment, flicked a speck of dust from his coat, opened and shut his snuff box, put it away, and growled, "Certainly. Good day, ma'am."

Charity was smiling calmly when Kate returned after hearing his lordship leave. "You made a great piece of work of that, Kate. I'm surprised at you. I realize he was not conciliating, but you have handled far touchier situations with more aplomb. And he was actually charming when he smiled that once. I explained the misunderstanding about Ralph's farm and agreed to convey his apologies."

Kate gave a reluctant chuckle. "I cannot say why he exasperates me so. It is the lingering doubts over Carl, no doubt. I suppose somewhere in me I still feel at fault, and I do not like to be with someone else who believes it, too."

"It was all very sad, my dear, but you have nothing with which to reproach yourself. Come, tell me what one wears for a skating party."

6

The next day while Kate sat with the cook to discuss the menu for the dinner after the skating and Susan went through her wardrobe to choose the costume which would most suit her coloring, Charity walked in the winter garden, where she was joined by Ralph.

"You met my sister in Daventry," he began awkwardly.

"Yes. We were great friends there. Of course, Kate was often travelling with your aunt, but they spent a good deal of time in town, too."

"Kate doesn't talk much about her travels."

"Perhaps because you don't ask her," Charity suggested gently.

Ralph flushed slightly. "No, well, why should I? I've never been anywhere."

"I should think, then, that you would be especially interested. Have you no desire to travel?"

"I guess not. Don't know. Never been anywhere but London."

"I was always fascinated by Kate's tales of Paris and Edinburgh and Dublin. She's had so many funny things happen to her. At least, when she talks of them they are amusing."

"Like what?"

"Oh, I could not tell them as she can. You should ask her."

"Perhaps I will."

"I have been tempted to envy Kate her adventures," Charity admitted thoughtfully, "but then, it's so much more enjoyable to simply share them with her." She gave a shiver as the chill wind blew through the garden.

"Here. You're cold. I shall take you in. Didn't mean to keep you outside talking until you caught your death," Ralph apologized.

The day of the skating party dawned cold and sparkling clear. Kate and Charity went down to the pond early to check the depth of the ice and returned chilled to report that all was well. A bleak sun shone through the wintry clouds as the time for the party approached. A roaring fire was built not far from the pond and benches were carried from the garden for seats. The servants arrived with steaming pitchers of hot chocolate and mulled wine, a vast assortment of tempting pastries, and an array of cold meats.

The three young ladies from the Hall arrived early with Mr. and Mrs. Montgomery and Ralph. Kate wore a fur-trimmed, deep blue mantelet and carried a matching fur muff of moderate size. Susan, on the other hand, had an enormous muff, a green cloak with a triple collar and wide cuffs with lace ruffles. Her blond ringlets escaped from a poke bonnet with three ostrich plumes. Charity's scarlet redingote was trimmed with gold frogging, and she had borrowed a beaverskin muff from Kate. The chill in the air had lifted somewhat, but their faces were pink with the cold and excitement.

As their guests arrived, the grooms led their horses

off to the warm stables and skates were donned immediately by the young people. Geoffrey Tolbert arrived with Terence Marsh and his brother and two sisters. Benjamin Karst and his sister Selina arrived next, closely followed by Lord Norris. This completed the party—a group of young men and women who had known each other since their earliest days, except for Selina and Benjamin Karst.

Kate had not seen Terence Marsh or Geoffrey Tolbert since their proposals to her, but she found them slightly embarrassed in her presence and made a point of putting them at their ease. They were grateful to her, and each took an opportunity to mumble a veiled apology.

Ralph was inclined to hover about Charity, but Kate made sure that her friend was introduced to everyone. Charles was determined to prove his newly acquired dignity to Susan, a feat which he accomplished by allowing her to circulate amongst the party yet being on hand to take her for refreshment when she required it. The laughter and chatter echoed about the pond, mingling with the crackle of the fire and the windsong soft in the wood. Kate surveyed the scene with pleasure. Benjamin Karst skated along with her and talked of his and Ralph's plans for breeding horses.

"Your father has spoken with mine, and they are agreeable to lending the necessary blunt if we will run the farm profitably as we get into the breeding. I think Drew will accept our offer, though Lord Winterton is interested in the property, too. Drew knows your father well and is inclined to frown on Winterton. That should help us! I hope we can depend on you for advice, Kate. Not on the horses, you understand," he hastened to add, "but on the farming. You seem to know a lot about it."

"I shall help all I can, Benjamin. I see no reason why the two of you should not make a go of it," Kate replied.

When Ralph saw an opportunity to detach Charity from the young people about her, he did so, which made her look about nervously for Kate, only to find her occupied in her discussion with Benjamin.

"We don't have a skating party very often," Ralph offered by way of conversation. "Such a cold winter should be used to advantage, don't you think?"

"Yes, I find it a lovely idea, and your sisters arranged it so skillfully."

"Oh, that's Kate. Susan simply does what she's told; Kate is the organizer. I imagine since your father is a vicar, you assist him with his parishioners, and I dare say they are grateful to have such an angel come to their aid." Ralph, who was not accustomed to dispensing compliments, delivered this one rather awkwardly.

Charity's normally placid countenance became slightly agitated. "I try to do what is necessary, Mr. Montgomery, for I adore my father and am always interested in his work. My mother and sisters and I are treated kindly by our neighbors."

When Charity stumbled on a patch of rough ice, Ralph quickly caught her hands to steady her, but instead of releasing them, he stared bemused into her face until she flushed and gasped, "Mr. Montgomery, I am quite all right now." She drew her hands from his in dismay when he did not seem to comprehend.

"Beg your pardon!" he gulped, realizing that he had upset her. "Here, shall I take you over to the fire?"

"No, thank you. I would like to speak with Kate a moment."

"Oh. I had hoped to have a chance to talk with you a while." His disappointment was so obvious that Charity could not bear to leave him standing there, but her invitation to him to escort her to Kate was issued diffidently. He was silent for a while as they skated across the pond. "Have I done something to offend you, Miss Martin-Smith? I would not for the world, you know. Why, I've never met a more beautiful, gentle creature than yourself, and I have nothing but admiration for you."

Charity stopped a pace away from Kate to face him. "I know you mean well, Mr. Montgomery, but I assure you I am not worthy of such notice. Miss Marsh, I believe, is skating too near the edge and you might warn her of the danger." She steeled herself to the hurt in his eyes, and with a sigh watched him move off to do her bidding.

Dinner was a noisy and cheerful occasion, followed by conversation, speculation and lottery tickets, and music. When the young people had finally departed for their homes, the Montgomerys and Charity sat enjoying tea and relaxing. As Mr. Montgomery engaged Ralph's attention, and Mrs. Montgomery and Susan were discussing the possibility that Lord Norris would be in London during the season, Kate took the opportunity to discuss with Charity a scheme which had been developing in her mind during the evening.

"I have been taking a break during your visit, Charity, from my plan to employ these young men usefully. I see some little success with Charles, and a bit with Ralph and Benjamin, but I am determined to turn my mind to the last two now. It occurs to me that politics might hold some interest for the Honourable Geoffrey Tolbert and Mr. Terence Marsh. What do you think?"

"Really, Kate, how should I know? Have either of them shown a preference in that direction?"

"That is why the idea occurred to me. They spent a great deal of time this evening talking about the Treaty of Paris and the Battle of New Orleans. I assure you each was quite convinced that he could have handled things better. And then they discussed the Corn Laws, too, and something about Bentham building an ideal prison, of all things. Perhaps they are no more interested than any other gentlemen in such things, but . . . I just cannot help feeling they have a *bent* for such an occupation," Kate said fervently, her eyes twinkling.

"You'll get yourself in trouble one day, Kate," her friend laughed. "How shall you go about it?"

"Their fathers are large landowners with no doubt more than one seat in their power. I cannot imagine how we shall get them interested, but no doubt something will occur to us."

"Us? You would involve me in your machinations, Kate? No, no. It is your affair, and I shall leave it to you. Besides, I shall only be here a few days more."

"Now that is another matter I had in mind to speak of with you. Is there any reason you must hurry back to Bath? Your sister is with your mother, and she cannot possibly need both of you. Will you not stay on with us for a while? I cannot tell you how much pleasure it gives me to have you here."

Ralph had been approaching them at this point and added his urging to that of his sister. Much to Kate's surprise, this appeared to make Charity more hesitant about accepting the invitation. When the rest of the family added their hopes of a prolonged stay, she agreed to write her mother next day. As Kate and Charity mounted the wide oak stairs, their candles slightly dispersing the dark, Kate could not help but ask, "Ralph has not been bothering you with his attentions, has he, Charity? I shall warn him off if you wish."

"No, no. He has been very kind to me, as you all have."

"You seemed to hesitate when he urged you to stay, it seemed to me. He is not much in the petticoat line, you know, and may be a bit awkward in his courting," Kate said with a smile.

"I do not want him to court me," Charity responded abruptly. "I feel sure his fancy will wane. He does not know me, after all."

"I cannot imagine but that the better he knows you, the more ardent he will become," Kate remarked seriously, trying to observe her friend's face in the candlelight. "Is it that you do not care for him, Charity? You may be plain with me."

"He has been everything that is kind to me, as has your entire family, but . . . Kate, I pray you will not meddle in this," Charity begged urgently.

"I promise I shall not. It is your own affair; forgive me for questioning you," Kate said contritely.

"I know it is only your concern for me which prompted you, Kate, and you must not think I am scolding you. You are a very dear friend, and I know you will allow me to handle my own life." Charity smiled. "Besides, you have quite enough to do just now without adding me to your list!

"You mock me, Charity. Sleep well, my dear."

A few days later a wintry sun invited some outdoor sport, and Kate offered to mount Charity on her favorite mare. While Kate and Susan were discussing a matter of local importance, Ralph rode ahead with Charity. He was eager to speak with her about the farm, his enthusiasm abbreviating his already terse style.

"Found the perfect horses to start with," he confided. "Winterton put us on to them. Had to go to Trowbridge, but it was worth it. Right price, too. Anyway, I might have had to go to Tattersall's, you know."

Charity smiled at his eagerness. "Lord Winterton is not resentful any longer, then? I thought he wished to purchase the farm himself."

"He did. But Benjamin ran into him one day, and Winterton just happened to mention the horses in Trowbridge. Didn't need them himself, you understand. Didn't cut him out or anything," he explained urgently.

"No, I'm sure you would not do such a thing," Charity replied.

"M' father wants us to farm the place for a profit, and Kate says she'll help with that. Good gun, Kate."

"Yes, and she seems to know a great deal about farming. Perhaps she can help you plan your course of study on the subject."

"My . . . oh, yes, to be sure," said the bewildered Ralph.

"Now that you are to own a property, no doubt you are anxious to learn how to go about making the best of it. It's quite an ambitious project, Mr. Montgomery, what with the farming and the breeding both unexplored territory. I admire your ambition."

Ralph could not be sure whether she was teasing him or whether she had merely picked up some of Kate's habits. He glanced at her glowing face, whipped to a high color by the wind, and was entranced by the trusting, doe-like eyes. Damn it, he thought ruefully, I would study archeology to justify her faith in me.

Kate was surprised when her brother approached her

on the matter of reading material about farming and breeding, but she supplied an overwhelming number of books and journals to him with alacrity. At his look of dismay she marked the most important texts and articles for a start. She was therefore not quite as shocked to learn that he had been talking with her father's tenants, but she did not discuss the matter with Charity, though she would have liked to know if this was the source of Ralph's sudden serious study of the subject.

She and her friend were riding back from the village one day when they came upon Ralph mounted on his horse, a small child seated behind him and clinging to his waist. Ralph was singing.

"My word!" Kate exclaimed involuntarily.

Ralph halted his song abruptly and explained sheepishly, "Found the little tyke in the wood. Gotten lost and hurt himself. One of the Jones brood, ain't he? I was taking him home."

"Yes," Kate agreed as she took in the tear-stained face. "You're Jeremy, aren't you? Feel better now?"

"Oh, yes, ma'am. Mr. Montgomery knows the funniest songs," the lad announced cheerfully.

"Does he? We shall have to have him sing them for us, won't we, Charity?" Kate asked with a wicked grin at her brother.

"Yes, indeed," Charity agreed as she bestowed a warm smile on Ralph, who flushed to the roots of his hair and said he must be off.

"He's fond of children and animals and has a remarkable knack with them." Kate remarked when the riders were beyond hearing. "I don't doubt that he'll do very well with his horses." She reined her horse toward the Hall and did not see the sad look in her friend's eyes as Charity watched Ralph's departing figure.

Ralph was pleased, if a trifle embarrassed, to be asked that evening by Charity to sing some of his songs for them. There was no difficulty for Kate in providing some background on the pianoforte for his rich baritone, though she was not always familiar with the tunes. He had to stop a moment before each, considering whether the words were appropriate to the present company, before he delighted them with various amusing pieces.

While he sang he was aware of Charity's eyes on him and he could have sworn that there was a special tenderness in them, but she would quickly bend down to set a stitch if he tried to meet her gaze. As his own reward for entertaining the family circle, he seated himself near her when Susan started to leaf through the music for a song she knew well enough to play.

"I must thank you for obliging me, Mr. Montgomery," Charity said softly. "You have a lovely voice and a charming repertoire."

"I always stop to listen when the village children are singing, though I didn't pick them all up that way," he confessed with a flush. "It is fascinating how the songs of the countryside are passed down from generation to generation. Children seem to absorb their heritage along with their daily bread. There must be great rewards in having a family, guiding young minds to knowledge and a sense of well-being, don't you think?"

Charity in her agitation pricked herself with a needle and sat gazing in alarm at the spot of blood Ralph dabbed from her finger. "Well, I . . . no . . . It seems to me that children are a very great responsibility. Not everyone is . . . prepared to undertake such a challenge. I myself cannot view it at all easily," she said with a valiant attempt at lightness. "Think of all the parents who despair of their offspring! I wonder whether it is worth the effort."

Ralph regarded her incredulously, and Charity did not give him an opportunity to respond, as she pointed out to him that Susan was ready to perform. Although it was difficult to ignore his obvious desire to continue their conversation, to understand her sentiments, she managed to devote her entire attention to Susan's uninspired playing and fell into discussion with the younger girl when she had concluded her recital. To Ralph she accorded only a smile before she retired to bed for the evening.

Several days later there were letters for most of the family. Charity received a missive from her mother, who was happy to have her daughter spend additional time at Montgomery Hall. She asked only that Charity return to Bath for the week before her own departure for Daventry.

Mrs. Montgomery received a pretty gilded sheet from her old and dear friend, Lady Stockton, who had found the perfect house for them to let during their London stay. Lady Stockton had originally insisted that Mrs. Montgomery and Susan stay with her, for she had visited them often, but Mr. Montgomery had been firm about their having a house of their own. He meant to accompany them to town and see them established before returning to the Hall.

Susan had a letter from Lady Stockton's daughter, Laura, who would be having her first season as well. Laura shared the London gossip and talked of the magnificent wardrobe she was acquiring, of the fittings and outings her mama took her on. The season would not begin for some time, but Laura was being quietly introduced to the *ton* by way of morning calls and informal evenings. "But you must not think that my head is entirely filled with these entertainments, dear Susan, for I continue my studies when there is time. I have conceived a passion for reading Shakespeare's plays, and to see them acted at the Theatre Royal is beyond my greatest dreams. You would scarcely credit it, but the majority of those who attend pay not the slightest attention to the work performed. They are all concerned with seeing and being seen," the young lady concluded scornfully.

Ralph received a message from Mr. Drew's solicitor advising him of the date his and Mr. Karst's purchase would be concluded. This sent him off to his studies once more.

The letter from Aunt Eleanor was addressed to Kate, but of course was intended for the entire family. She and Mr. Hall, whom she referred to as Dawson, were having a splendid time, had enjoyed the Alps and the Low Countries, but were beginning to think of returning to Daventry to pick up their lives there together. They intended to visit Montgomery Hall on their return. Kate laughed over the part which read, "Dawson makes quite as agreeable a travelling companion as you, my dear, and it is so very comfortable to have a man in charge, since people *listen* to men. I shall never forget the experience you and I had in Paris where the concierge would not understand our French until we had inveigled that dear Mr. Thompson to vouch for us." Dear Mr. Thompson, Kate remembered well. She had successfully foiled his attempts to assume the role of suitor and she had been much relieved when the colorful dandy had married a young woman from Nottingham and had settled there.

When the letter was read by Ralph he made a valiant effort, in Charity's presence, to draw Kate out on her travels. She was not loath to talk of them, for they were among her fondest memories. And although she might have been somewhat mystified by his sudden interest, his attention was everything it should have been. He even absently offered her snuff during her recital, so intent was he.

"No, thank you, Ralph," she demurred politely, and, seeing that he was about to do the same for Charity, continued, "I do not think Charity is in the habit of taking snuff, either."

"Sorry," he murmured, recollecting himself. "Didn't know what I was doing. Shame we don't do the Grand Tour anymore."

"I imagine more people will travel now that things are settling down in France," Charity suggested.

"Would you like to go there?" Ralph asked in such an eager way that it made Charity flush slightly.

"I doubt I shall ever get there, but I do enjoy hearing about it. And seeing your Aunt Eleanor's sketches makes everything come alive. I hope she will have them with her when she comes to visit you." Charity returned her gaze to the embroidery frame and simulated an intense concentration on her work there.

Ralph looked questioningly at Kate, but she was unable to help him. Kate recognized as well as he did that this was no shy maiden demurely hesitant to accept his advances. This was not the first time Kate had seen her friend keep her brother firmly at arm's length. Ralph soon excused himself and sought out his father over some detail involved in the purchase of the farm.

7

Kate and Charity spent the next week pleasantly taking walks, drives, and rides about the area when the weather permitted and sitting over embroidery frames talking when conditions outside were foul. It took some perseverance on Ralph's part to find Kate alone, but he did so late one afternoon. She was in the back parlor playing a dulcimer she had found years ago in the attic. As he was hesitant about the subject he wished to broach, he waited patiently for her to finish a piece before beginning.

"I . . . I . . . it's about Charity," he blurted. When his sister regarded him inquiringly he continued, "Beautiful girl. Such a sweet disposition—always calm and pleasant. Quite fond of her." His face colored slightly.

"She is indeed the finest young woman of my acquaintance," Kate responded carefully.

"Yes, yes. To be sure. What I have been wondering is . . . well . . . has she spoken with you about me at all?"

His countenance was so gravely serious and concerned that Kate could not help but feel for him. "She has spoken kindly of you, as of the rest of the family." Kate could not find anything further to say which would comfort him and not betray her promise.

"And that is all? I had thought . . . that is, she seemed to like me well enough. We've laughed together and talked of my plans for the farm. But sometimes she's rather distant with me. I cannot think how I have offended her!"

"Now, Ralph, I doubt you have done so. Why do you not speak with her?"

"She's at some pains never to be alone with me," he said sadly. "I can hardly talk to her with you and Susan around. Could you arrange it so we should be alone together? Promise I would not force my attentions on her. Do you think her heart is engaged elsewhere?"

"Really, Ralph, I could not say. I am not in her confidence in such matters. You must make your own way in this. I should not interfere where my brother and my friend are involved," she replied with finality.

Ralph gave an exasperated shrug and wandered unhappily from the room. Kate stared after him, absently fingering the strings of the dulcimer. It had become obvious to her as well that Charity was attempting to avoid her brother, but she was at a loss to explain it. And of course she could not press Charity further. Her friend appeared to have a calming effect on Ralph which pleased Kate. There had been many rides about the countryside when she had observed the two together and been very pleased that they got on so well. But she must have been mistaken if Charity was indeed discouraging Ralph's attentions. It would not be the first time she had been mistaken, she thought ruefully, as she bent her attention to the dulcimer again.

When Ralph left Kate, he wandered through the house, aware that Charity was with Susan in the garden. He had been so excited about the scheme for the farm before Charity came, and his developing fond-

ness for her had led him to share with her some of his
plans and dreams. Charity had helped him translate
some of these into a more realistic form. At her suggestion, he had indeed delved into the mysteries of the
countryside, and he had proceeded to learn more for
his own benefit and not for the sake of outshining Lord
Winterton or even pleasing Charity.

His partner, Benjamin Karst, had at first been puzzled by Ralph's growing interest in technical matters
and had teased him unendingly. But he was loath to
set his ignorance against Ralph's growing knowledge,
and he secretly began to study the subject as well.
Benjamin and Ralph were to conclude the purchase of
the farm on the following day, and Ralph was anxious
to push for some enlightenment on Charity's feelings.
So he bribed a footman to call Susan away from the
garden on an imaginary errand and, with hands
clasped nervously behind his back, approached Charity, who was seated in the arbor.

"Miss Martin-Smith, I would beg a word with you,"
he began.

Charity's natural poise did not desert her, for she
had realized that this moment must come, but in-
wardly she quaked at what she must do. "Mr. Montgomery, do be seated. Can I assist you in some way?"
she asked, her manner not at all encouraging.

"I have come to cherish the highest regard for you,
Miss Martin-Smith . . . Charity. May I call you so?"

"As it pleases you."

"I had hoped that you might return my regard," he
continued anxiously.

"I am sure I regard you as a most congenial companion and friend," Charity replied stiffly.

"I don't want to be your friend," he sighed unhappily. "That is, I want to make you my wife."

Charity's countenance remained placid, but lost some of its usual color. "Mr. Montgomery . . . Ralph . . . do not say so. You can scarce know me after a few weeks in the same house. You and your family have been so kind to me. I feel sure you are mistaken in your feelings, though I am honored by your interest in me. I must tell you that I have no intention of marrying ever, Ralph, though I would beg you not to speak of that to anyone, even Kate. I shall . . . always hold you in the greatest affection." Charity rose abruptly and turned her back to him so that he would be unable to see her swiftly brush away the tear that escaped.

Ralph rose, too, and stood helplessly gazing at her back. "I had hoped we could have a home of our own, build a modest house on the farm, or live on the estate near Rugby," he said despondently.

"Say no more, I beg you," she gasped, digging in her reticule for the wisp of lace which must serve to stem the flow of tears which she could no longer withhold.

"I've distressed you!" Ralph cried, mortified, as he saw her furtively put the handkerchief to her eyes. "Wouldn't do so for the world! Forgive me! I'm the clumsiest of fellows." He distractedly forced his hand through his thick blond hair, making it stand on end.

Charity turned to soothe his agitation, and a hysterical desire to laugh at the sight of his upright hair checked the flow of her tears. He looked so forlorn in his despair that her already overburdened heart could take no more, and she fled without another word. Ralph watched her retreat in numb hopelessness. He finally gathered his wits about him enough to head for the stables.

'My curricle, Harris," he ordered absently, "with

the bays.'' When this vehicle was ready, he asked, ''Should be a full moon tonight, what?''

''Yes, a fine evening,'' Harris responded as he stood patiently at the horses' heads.

''I shall go alone. Send word to the Hall that I may spend the night at Mr. Karst's.''

''Very good, sir,'' the groom replied. He could see that Mr. Montgomery was upset, and it would no doubt be wiser for him to stay the night with his friend if he were in his cups, as Harris felt sure he would be.

But it was not Ralph's plan that he should spend the evening with Benjamin before a warming fire, a glass of brandy in his hand. It had occurred to him that they had too long put off their night race to Bath and back. The weather appeared likely to hold; there was no sign of fresh snow. The dull gray sky surmounted a landscape deep frozen with no sign of thaw. Although the roads were rutted and uneven from the previous thaw and freeze, they were perfectly negotiable; there was little chance of a curricle being mired down.

Ralph found Benjamin in the library, studying some literature on horse breeding. They spent some time discussing their plans before Ralph suggested that their race be held that very evening.

''I thought you'd forgotten it,'' Benjamin declared. ''It's been difficult to get you away from the Hall these last few weeks.''

''I hadn't forgotten. Tonight should be a full moon. May not have better for months. Are you game?''

Benjamin smiled widely. ''You're on. Still fifty guineas?''

''Yes, to the Nowland farm, turn, and back here. Start at ten?''

''So late?''

"Should be less traffic then, but it makes no difference to me."

"Ten it shall be. You stay to dine, of course."

Their race was conducted over a course of rutted, winding country lanes by the light of a pale full moon. The lead changed several times in spite of the narrow way, with first Benjamin's scarlet and then Ralph's blue curricle in the fore. Across deserted fields to avoid a flock of geese, or swinging around a bend at high speed, the two young men called to one another cheerfully or sang at the tops of their voices. For this short space of time Ralph could involve himself in the race and thrust aside his despondent thoughts. On the return journey Benjamin was in the lead and Ralph saw his last chance of overtaking him as they approached a bend wide enough for both curricles. His mood had become reckless, and while Benjamin took the turn cautiously, Ralph determined to make his move before his bays flagged entirely. Around the bend he heard only the slightest touching of the wheel against the bank, and he steadied his horses onto the stretch ahead. But he had not been able to see the road ahead, and he was suddenly faced with a country lad unconcernedly plodding along on his old nag. Ralph cursed wildly as he tried to bring the bays to the side of the road.

Although he managed to avoid doing the lad and his horse a mischief, his leader stumbled and the already swaying curricle was flung against the bank of the road. Benjamin watched horrified as Ralph was flung from the curricle against the bank and onto the road. The bays stumbled to a shuddering halt while Benjamin dexterously skirted the accident and drew in his own team. He leaped to the ground even as they slowed and raced to his friend. He found Ralph in pain but conscious.

"Are you all right?" Benjamin asked anxiously.

"Don't know. See to the horses, will you?"

"When I've had a look at you. Can you get up?"

"Can't be sure. Give me a hand and I'll try." But Ralph gasped with agony as he tried to rise, and his arm hung limply at his side. His face was scraped and muddy, his clothes (including Benjamin's borrowed driving coat) torn, and his hat gone. "Leave me a minute and see to the horses," he begged.

Benjamin returned to tell him that the wheeler was lame but that no bones appeared to be broken. "Your curricle is a mess, the wheel smashed and the axle damaged, too, I think, though it is difficult to see in this poor light."

"God, I'm an idiot. I should know better than to come round a blind corner like that."

"Bad luck. You'd have made it if it hadn't been for that lad." This person was still sitting astride his horse, staring at the confusion in the road. He made no remark and no attempt to help.

"Can you get me to your curricle?" Ralph asked.

Benjamin surveyed the taller man dubiously. When he had made an unsuccessful attempt, he called to the lad to give him a hand. This seemed to inspire the fellow to dig his heels into his horse, which startled that sluggish beast so much that he took off at a trot. Benjamin returned his attention to his companion and was considerably shaken when another voice met his ears. He had not been aware that anyone else was on the scene, and had thought the hoofbeats he heard were those of the departing lad.

"What now?" the Earl of Winterton asked wearily, surveying the disorder with a jaundiced eye.

"Ralph has smashed his curricle, and I could use some help to get him to mine, Lord Winterton," Benjamin explained.

"Broken anything, Montgomery?" Winterton asked as he leisurely dismounted.

"How should I know?" Ralph flared. "I can't stand, and my left arm is useless."

"It's better than being dead," Winterton remarked roughly. "I gather you two fools were racing." He unfastened the driving coat and probed Ralph's arms and legs to the accompaniment of the younger man's stifled grunts of pain. "Legs are probably only sprained, but the arm is broken. Give me a hand, Karst, and we'll put him in your curricle." When this had been accomplished, Ralph gritting his teeth the while, Winterton continued, "Take him to the Manor."

"That will not be necessary, Lord Winterton," Benjamin retorted stiffly. "I shall take him home with me. Thank you for your assistance."

"The Manor is half a mile and your home not much less than three," the Earl mused. "If you are lucky, he will faint shortly from the pain and the additional distance will then not matter to him, of course. The arm should be set immediately." Winterton mounted his horse, nodded to the two young men, and rode off.

"Haughty bastard!" Benjamin exclaimed as he gave his horses the office to start. Ralph's gasp at the movement caused his friend to survey him critically, noting the pallor of his forehead and cheeks. "Shall it be the Manor?" he asked gruffly.

"Yes," Ralph sighed.

They turned down the lane after Winterton, who had of course, assumed they would follow and proceeded to the Manor stables. When they arrived he had completed arrangements for removing Ralph's curricle and horses from the road to his own stables. He had already issued orders to two sleepy grooms; one to fetch the doctor and another to inform the housekeeper that a bedroom on the ground floor should be prepared immediately. Ralph was carried into the great hall, across the black and white marble floor and through a maze of corridors which ran past the breakfast room, the china room, and the map room until the West Room was finally reached, much to his relief. He was deposited on the bed, while the housekeeper watched from the doorway.

"Has Thomas been awakened by the bustle, Mrs. Pettit?" Winterton asked her.

"Yes, my lord. He's in the library."

"Good. Send him to me, and have Crocker bring a nightshirt and some brandy for Mr. Montgomery, please."

Thomas Single, Lord Winterton's secretary, arrived almost immediately and stood slightly smiling in the doorway. "Just a quiet evening in Bristol," he murmured.

Winterton grinned at him and said, "Mind your manners, Thomas. I think you know Mr. Montgomery and Mr. Karst. It seems they had an accident while racing. It was just our good fortune that it should occur so close," he remarked mournfully. "Would you send a note to the Montgomerys assuring them that there is no dire threat to Ralph and that a doctor has been sent for?" As the young man turned to leave he added, "And, Thomas, make it plain that I do not wish to have a gaggle of females descend on me in the middle of the night. Suggest ten in the morning as an appropriate time for anyone to call."

"Certainly, Lord Winterton," Thomas replied, re-pressing a smile.

Ralph attempted to raise himself, gave up the effort with a wince, and said, "You need not inform them until the morning, Lord Winterton. They do not expect me back tonight."

"All the better. Arrange for the note to be sent off in the morning then, Thomas."

"Certainly, sir."

The valet, Crocker, arrived next with brandy and a nightshirt. After Ralph had been supported for a few sips, Winterton directed his valet to undress and clean the young man of his mud. Winterton led Benjamin to the White Parlor and offered him a drink, which the young man gladly accepted. "Shall I have a room made ready for you, Karst?" he asked courteously.

"Thank you, no, sir. I shall just stay until the doctor has seen Ralph, if you don't mind."

"As you wish, though it may be some time before he arrives. I understand the two of you are purchasing the Drew farm with some idea of breeding horses."

"Yes," Benjamin replied stiffly, aware that Lord Winterton had hoped to purchase the farm himself. He braced himself for the sharp edge of his host's tongue but was surprised instead to find himself regaled with an account of the mishaps and mistakes Winterton had made when he started his own venture. He was even more surprised when Winterton offered him some sound advice, not at all patronizingly, and had his secretary bring some books and articles for him before sending Thomas off to bed.

"That must be the doctor now," Winterton remarked as the sound of voices in the hall reached them. The two men accompanied the doctor, an older man with wild white hair worn long and tied back with a

black ribbon, to the patient's room. Ralph was resting
reasonably comfortably, but it was fortunate that he
fainted early in the setting of his arm, for it was a most
painful enterprise. Benjamin assisted as best he could
in spite of the dizziness he began to feel. When the
ordeal was over, Winterton thrust him in a chair and
urged a glass of brandy on him. This restored him
sufficiently to take his leave of Winterton and find his
way home.

When the room was cleared of all but Winterton,
his valet, and the now-sleeping patient, Winterton remarked wryly, "He'll waken with pain in a few hours.
I'll sit by to give him some laudanum if he needs it."
He roamed about the room for a moment and commented absently, "He was Carl's best friend." Re-
calling himself, he addressed Crosby rather curtly,
"You may go now. I shall not need you further tonight."

The valet bowed and closed the door softly behind
himself. Winterton stood gazing out the window for
some time before lowering himself wearily onto a
velvet-covered chair not really large enough to seat
him comfortably, but the best the room had to offer.
He dozed fitfully while Ralph tossed and groaned,
every movement of his body causing him pain. He
awoke only once and in a daze accepted some water
and a few drops of laudanum, which helped him spend
a more peaceful night.

Winterton awoke early, checked the patient for fe-
ver, and, finding none, departed for his room, sending
a footman in his stead. He found Crosby already patiently awaiting him and smiled companionably at the
older man. "I think I could use a ride to clear my
head. I should see that there is a more comfortable
chair put in the West Room."

"As you say, my lord. I would have sat with him."

"I know," Winterton replied wearily. "He's not a bad fellow—very like Carl, really. He just wants a bit of responsibility to make him take hold."

8

Kate walked in to breakfast to find her father reading a note, his brow drawn in a frown. "What is it, Papa? Not bad news?"

"Certainly not the best I've had this week. It's from Winterton's secretary informing me that Ralph has been injured in a curricle accident, but is in no danger. They were calling in the doctor." He lifted his eyes to his daughter, then read, " 'As Mr. Montgomery will no doubt require a great deal of rest after his accident, it is suggested that his family call no earlier than ten.' " He chuckled appreciatively. "No doubt my Lord Winterton does not wish to be overrun before he breakfasts."

"I doubt he arises so early," Kate said scornfully, but returned her father's twinkle. "Shall we all go? It would serve his lordship right."

"Your mama does not know of this as yet. Let us not worry her unnecessarily. Finish your breakfast, and we'll drive over together."

It lacked but a few minutes to ten when Mr. Montgomery and his daughter arrived at Winter Manor. They were shown into the White Parlor, where Lord Winterton joined them immediately. "Sir, Miss Montgomery, your servant. Ralph is badly bruised and has broken an arm, but I assure you he is mending already.

He consumed a truly remarkable breakfast.'' He smiled charmingly at them.

Kate could not help returning his smile. "May we see him now?''

Her father raised an admonitory hand. "We have not thanked his lordship yet, my dear. We are once again in your debt, Lord Winterton. How did the accident come about?''

"He probably drove Ralph off the road,'' Kate murmured, to her father's astonishment and Winterton's amusement.

"Not this time, I assure you, Miss Montgomery. I found your brother had had an accident but a short distance from my gates. I'll take you to him, and he can answer your questions himself.''

As he led them through the house, Mr. Montgomery regarded his daughter with a puzzled frown. Winterton left them alone with Ralph as soon as they entered the room. Kate hastened to her brother's side to avoid the question on her father's tongue. "How are you feeling, Ralph?''

"I've been better,'' he grumbled with a crooked smile.

"What happened?''

"Benjamin and I were having a race. Tried to overtake him on a corner, more fool I. Made it all right, you understand, but I had to pull over quickly to avoid a horse and rider. Horses stumbled. M' curricle was thrown into a bank and I was tossed out. Most undignified. Winterton came along after a bit and here I am. Dr. Armitage set the arm, I remember, though I fainted before he finished.''

"That was fortunate,'' his father grunted. "I thought you had given up such pastimes, Ralph. Racing at night in the dead of winter, indeed! Perhaps Dr.

Armitage should examine your head," he suggested sarcastically.

"I admit it was foolish, Father. It was just . . ." Ralph's face became suddenly sad and he finished lamely, "just a lark."

"I shall enjoy telling your mother so," his father retorted.

"Can we take you home, Ralph?" Kate interjected.

"Winterton says Dr. Armitage suggested I stay here a day or two. My bruises and arm do not take well to a jolting. But I dare say I could manage it," he proclaimed stoutly.

"There's no need to rack your body about," Mr. Montgomery stated gruffly. "I'm sure Winterton won't mind you here for a day."

"No, indeed," Kate said. "I am sure he must be the perfect host."

"Well, as to that, Kate, you should know that he stayed here with me last night. I thought it very obliging of him."

"I think it astonishing," she returned pertly.

"What did I do to deserve such skip-brains for children?" Mr. Montgomery lamented. "Winterton is excessively proud, to be sure, but he is also a remarkably intelligent and generous man. We have seen examples enough of his kindness in our family to overlook his manner, surely. I expect both of you to treat him respectfully in future. Am I understood?"

"Yes, sir," they replied in unison.

"Excellent! We must go and advise your mama of this latest scrape, Kate. No doubt she will call to see you this afternoon, son. She can bring any necessities."

On their way out of the room they were intercepted by Mr. Single, who advised them that Lord Winterton would welcome their waiting on him in the library. He was frowning over a document when they entered, but readily dropped it and greeted them. "I hope you have found Ralph in satisfactory condition. Dr. Armitage suggested he spend a day or so here, and I trust you will avail yourselves of my home. No doubt Mrs. Montgomery will call this afternoon."

"We are grateful to accept. Ralph says you sat with him yourself last night. That was extremely kind of you," Mr. Montgomery remarked.

Kate was intrigued to see that this remark clearly embarrassed Winterton.

"I am surprised he remembers," Winterton finally conceded with a smile. "He had a restless night, but he appeared to have less pain this morning."

"I only hope he has learned a lesson," Mr. Montgomery opined.

"Forever optimistic, sir?" his host queried.

Mr. Montgomery laughed. "Always. I regret I may not live to watch *you* raise a brood, Winterton. Don't bother to see us out. We are imposing on your hospitality quite sufficiently already."

But Winterton insisted on seeing them out and then returned to look in on Ralph. He surprised the young man staring miserably at his hands and, in an effort to cheer him said, "You'll be up in no time, Ralph. Feeling rotten?"

"Yes. That is, no, I feel much better this morning."

"Your father ring a peal over you?"

"Yes," Ralph grinned. "Told Kate and me that we should treat you with respect. Sorry if I've been churlish. I took exception to your interfering in my horse trading some weeks back, though you were right, of course. Don't hold my brandy well, I fear."

Winterton surveyed the young man for some time

before replying. "I was used to looking out for you and Carl when you were younger. I have no right to interfere with you, and I do not blame you for being annoyed. But I hope you will feel free to call on me for advice about the farm if there is anything I can help with."

Ralph sighed and mumbled, "Thank you, sir. The farm has lost its attraction for me."

Winterton eyed him sharply. "Since when? Karst spoke enthusiastically last night of the preparations you are both making. I made sure you were as eager as he to have a go at it. You won't be in bed long."

"It's not that. There was another hope I cherished, and it has been dashed. What good will the farm be now?"

"There never was anything like work to take one's mind off a sorrow," Winterton replied softly.

"How would you know?" Ralph spoke angrily, waving his injured fist unwisely. He recalled himself sharply and said penitently, "I am a fool. Forgive me, Winterton. I must be totally distracted."

Winterton regarded him with tolerant exasperation. He had no doubt that Ralph was talking about a woman, and the only candidate he could picture was that gentle creature Miss Montgomery had introduced into the Hall. How the spitfire had ever become friends with such a composed, patient soul strained his imagination. "You might ask your sister's help," he suggested.

"Kate refuses to meddle," Ralph said disgustedly.

"Then it must be the first time," Winterton retorted and rose to leave his guest.

Kate and her father arrived at the Hall while the rest of the family was still in the breakfast room. Kate happened to glance at Charity as her father was explaining Ralph's accident and injuries. Charity's face paled alarmingly and Kate was about to rush to her when a sixth sense warned her that it would not be wise to do so. Instead she urged, "Charity, would you come with me to see the cook? I would like to send Ralph a special treat with Mama."

"That is kind of you, dear," her mother commented distractedly. "I shall of course take everything necessary when I go to call. Shall I take some elixir? Is it warm in his room? Does he have a warm nightshirt? He will need his dressing gown, of course."

As Mrs. Montgomery rattled off the list she intended to take, Kate caught Charity's arm and ushered her out of the room. Instead of heading for the kitchen, she led her friend into the book room and sat her on a comfortable couch.

"Can I get you a vinaigrette? I'm sure I must have one in my dressing table."

"No, no. I shall be fine in a moment," Charity replied faintly.

Kate smiled encouragingly. "Ralph is really not so very bad, you know. He will have a lot of aches and bruises for a while, but nothing that will not mend. I cannot say that he was in much pain when we saw him."

"Why would he do such a thing? Racing at night must be very hazardous. He might have been killed!"

"But he was not. Oh, there had been talk of such a race some time ago, but I felt sure that he and Benjamin were much too involved in the farm to give it any thought. Perhaps it was a last fling before settling in to the farm."

"He asked me to marry him yesterday, Kate, and I

refused him," Charity said very softly, as she twisted her sash with nervous hands.

"Well, I am sorry to hear it. I should love to have you for my sister, and it is plain to see that Ralph is very attached to you. But I promised you I would not meddle, and so I shall not." With an effort Kate put aside her disappointment and smiled at her friend. "Do you feel up to invading the kitchen with me? Or would you rather stay here a bit?"

"I feel better now."

"Then come with me, for if we leave it to Mama the hamper that goes will consist of broth and possets, when Ralph would much rather, I am sure, have some cinnamon tarts and Chantilly cake."

Mrs. Montgomery subsequently drove off with Susan in the barouche with enough food and clothing to last her suffering firstborn for a week. Kate saw to it that Charity was not invited to join the party; she improvised an important errand for the two of them in the village on Ralph's behalf.

There was an awkward silence between the two young women when the carriage had left and they started walking along the frozen lane. Charity was the first to speak.

"You are not angry with me for refusing Ralph, are you?"

"How can you ask such a question? I would have to by a hypocrite to be so. My dear, I want you to do just what you must to be happy," Kate assured her firmly.

At this Charity burst into tears, much to Kate's astonishment. She led her friend into the woods and seated her on a fallen log. "Do you cry for hurting Ralph? You are too sensitive, my love. He is a bit spoiled and is used to having just what he pleases. I have never known him to be interested in a woman before, and this will be a blow for him. But, Charity, he is my father's son, and I think there is a strength there under his careless exterior. Wipe your tears. He shall come about.''

This advice did not ease the ache in Charity's heart, but she dutifully wiped her eyes and attempted a tremulous smile. Kate regarded her closely and noted the pain in her eyes. Why, she loves Ralph, she thought in amazement. It was not amazing to her that someone should love her brother, of course, for she was extremely fond of him herself, in spite of the fact that he exasperated her frequently. But she could not conceive of any reason for her friend to refuse Ralph if she loved him. They were not of unequal stations or even fortunes, for Charity had a reasonable inheritance from her great-aunt. But Kate had promised not to interfere, and it was no more than she should expect, she thought grimly, to be handicapped just when she most wished to help. That Charity would not confide in her was upsetting. It might have to do with Ralph's being her brother, but more likely it was that Charity knew her to be forever managing the lives of those around her. Kate felt suddenly ashamed and hugged her friend impulsively, and said, ''Forgive me.''

Charity blinked her eyes in bewilderment. ''Forgive you for what?''

''For being . . . oh, just me.''

''But you are my dearest friend and I love you.''

''You must find it difficult at times.'' Kate was afraid that if she said any more her friend would feel forced to confide in her against her will. ''Come, we shall go into the village and look for something to cheer up the invalid. And I am in need of some stockings. We shall indulge ourselves and have tea at the Unicorn.''

When they had managed to dispense with their errands—Kate purchasing blue stockings just for the fun of it—they wandered to the inn and were directed into the public parlor. Here they found Mrs. Marsh and Lady Tolbert, who invited the young women to join them.

"The young people enjoyed your skating party, my dear," Mrs. Marsh assured Kate, "though it tempted them to do some skating on their own, which did not end so well. James chased Mary over onto some thin ice, and they both took quite a dip. Fortunately Lord Norris had been watching them and immediately came to their rescue, though I fear he had quite a time of it getting them both out, soaked as they were. Neither contracted the slightest cold from it, which I must ascribe to his quick action.''

"I'm glad they took no harm. Lord Norris had not mentioned the escapade.'' This in itself impressed Kate, for he had formerly dramatized events and called to Susan's attention any action worthy of merit. Such self-restraint surely deserved that Kate inform her sister of his heroism, which would delight Susan.

Mrs. Marsh proceeded to inform her auditors that her children enjoyed the most exuberant health, and that James had a scolding for his part. "But he is not one to worry over such matters.'' Mrs. Marsh smiled indulgently, wagging a turbaned head. "I shall be relieved when they reach Terence's age and outgrow such mischievous behavior,'' she sighed, and took a bite from one of the three biscuits on her plate.

Kate and Charity shared an ironic glance, considering Terence Marsh's part in the recent prank, but Kate, who had planned to drop a word in the ear of

Mrs. Marsh or Lady Tolbert concerning the possibility of brilliant futures for their sons in politics, remained demurely silent. It was obvious that the two older women had not heard of the episode of the five suitors, and naturally they were not enlightened. So the four women enjoyed a comfortable tea and shared the local gossip over tasty scones and biscuits.

Charity drew her green pelisse about her against the chilly wind when they emerged from the Unicorn. She regarded Kate quizzingly and said, "Did you not just pass up the most golden opportunity for promoting the political careers of the Honourable Geoffrey Tolbert and Mr. Terence Marsh?"

"I have decided to give up meddling," Kate sighed sadly. "No good can come of it."

"Nonsense," Charity retorted briskly. "You are very good at it, you know, and you should not hide your light under a bushel." She laughingly eyed her friend as Kate shifted the packages from one arm to the other. "My dear, you have a knack of pointing people in the right direction without lecturing them or scolding them. Do not tell me I have discouraged you from your pursuits! I enjoy them enormously," she admitted frankly.

"Do you? But you would not have me meddle in your affairs," Kate responded unhappily.

"I would not have you pity me," Charity retorted cryptically, and changed the subject.

9

The Earl of Winterton bore with equanimity his neighbor's stay at Winter Manor. He was pleasant to Mrs. Montgomery and Susan when they called, and he even went so far as to take his dinner in the West Room with Ralph, conversing easily on matters of farming and breeding which might interest his guest. When Benjamin Karst called in the evening at a rather unorthodox hour, explaining that it had taken him the whole of the day to soothe and placate his family, the Earl merely smiled reminiscently and showed him to the invalid's room.

Ralph was impatient to be back at the Hall and departed eagerly if painfully with his father in the well-sprung carriage at ten the next morning. The Montgomerys' various expressions of thanks were casually accepted, and the Earl himself stood at the door until the carriage was out of sight.

"Making sure he's gone, sir?"

The Earl turned around lazily toward his secretary, who was doing his best to smother a smile. "That is precisely what I was doing, Thomas. How acute of you. I presume you wish to drag me off to your office to discuss the price of chickens or the latest destruction of a tenant's roof."

"Something of that nature, sir, if you have a moment."

"Not above half an hour, Thomas. I have been housebound for quite long enough, I assure you. I was expected in Bristol last night, and I shall have a bit of work of it to explain my absence and cajole the young lady into a pleasant frame of mind."

"You could have sent a message, sir."

"Yes, Thomas, I could have, but I did not feel like it," Winterton remarked as he swung his quizzing glass absently back and forth.

"As you say, sir. Is my half-hour ticking away?" he asked with an impudent grin.

"It is."

"Then with all due respect let me usher you to my office."

Winterton did not manage to leave the Manor for over an hour. Thomas Single was grateful for this, since it meant that he was able to deal with several matters which had arisen suddenly and urgently. Winterton, on the other hand, felt slightly oppressed and could not put a finger on his restlessness. A pair of high-spirited chestnuts awaited his pleasure, and he gathered the reins in his hands, jumped into the curricle, and ordered, "Let 'em go, Peters."

The freshness of the horses demanded all his attention for a while, and he was not quite in the proper mood to notice that the late-February sun was likely to foretell the first of spring. There was a persistent dripping in the countryside about him as the thaw began in the frozen land. The brooks and streams would soon swell to bursting as the ice and snow reluctantly disappeared for another year. The hunting season would end now, and his restlessness would not be assuaged by the pseudo-French lady in Bristol. Celeste had soon lost her attraction for him, and he would do well perhaps to head for London for the more sophisticated women to be found there who would welcome his patronage. At least one could find a little wit and humor amongst the demimonde there, rather than the petulant, insistent demands of Celeste in Bristol.

Responsibility had never weighed upon Winterton regarding his duty to marry and beget an heir for Winter Manor. There were cousins enough to fill that role if need be; not that he ever made the least push to make the acquaintance of the half of them. The heir apparent was an unprepossessing elderly man, and Lord Norris himself was not so very far away in the succession, considering the age of those in line ahead of him.

Winterton drove his chestnuts, the edge now off them, into the crowded inn yard just as the Bath & Bristol Express Coach arrived. He was not forgotten in the ensuing bustle, as he was a well-known figure there. An ostler took charge of the curricle and was informed, in the most off-hand manner, that his lordship had no idea when he would return for it. Winterton strode out of the inn yard at his usual brisk pace and was soon at the gabled cottage in Small Street where his mistress was housed. His imperative rap at the door brought a seedy-looking servant to the door without visible haste.

"Tell Celeste that Lord Winterton is here," he ordered, setting his gloves and cane on a side table which needed to be dusted and had seen better days. He did not know this servant and wondered idly if Celeste had dismissed the suitably discreet employee he had provided for her.

The servant shambled off without a word and shambled back some ten minutes later to inform his lordship in a grunt that he would be admitted. "I know the way," he informed the lackey, momentarily considering the wisdom of leaving his gold-headed cane and tan leather driving gloves in the keeping of such a shifty-eyed fellow. But he had other matters on his mind and could not be bothered with such a trifle. As he had expected, he found Celeste in her boudoir scantily clothed in a flimsy gauze grown of sea green.

Popping a bonbon into her pouting red mouth, she said accusingly, "I expected you last night."

"I was unable to come."

"You said you would," she pressed.

"But I didn't. I hope your waiting for me did not cause you any inconvenience," he returned softly.

"Well, it was a great bore, I assure you."

"I am here now and you need no longer be bored," he suggested, "though you certainly still appear to be so."

Celeste did not miss the snap in his voice and the angry flicker in his eyes. She elegantly unwrapped herself from the luxurious fourposter and approached him seductively. "Shall I ring for wine?" she purred.

"If you think that shifty-eyed beggar can manage it."

She gave a tinkling laugh as she tugged at the bell pull. "He's right quick with the wine, as it gives him a chance to sample it."

Winterton grimaced with disgust and pulled her onto his lap as he seated himself on the bed. He began to caress her carelessly, and she took the opportunity to suggest that she needed a new gown. It had become a ritual to make demands of her lover in the early stages of each encounter, since his invariable response was "Perhaps, if you please me." There was a scratch on the door, and the servant entered when bidden, avert-

ing his eyes, and set a tray with decanter and glass on
the draped dressing table. He vanished immediately,
and Celeste rose to pour out a glass for Winterton.

"You don't join me?"

"Not today, Andrew."

She rejoined him on the bed, and he continued to
fondle her as he sipped at his wine, moodily staring
off into space. Celeste was pricked by this indiffer-
ence, but it had become not an unusual feature of their
lovemaking. She smiled secretly and decided that her
course of action had been perfectly justified. He was
tired of her, and what was a working girl to do but
make the best of a bad situation?

When Winterton finished the wine, he set the glass
carefully on the old-fashioned night commode and
turned his attention to his companion. His interest was
increasing, but now his head began to feel muddled
and his actions started to take on a nightmarish slow-
motion quality. He fought to shake off the sluggish-
ness, but he felt confused and powerless. Perhaps if
he just lay still for a moment he would be better. There
was an angry flash of understanding just before he lost
consciousness.

When Winterton awoke, his head felt like a balloon
and his eyes took some time to function properly. He
was aware of the gray light outside and could not at
first remember where he was. He lay on a fourposter
bed, he observed, and nearby was a night commode
with a short flight of steps. Certainly he was not at
Winter Manor. Turning his head was an agony, but he
proceeded to take in the mahogany tallboy, the dainty
writing bureau, the draped dressing table and the swing
looking-glass. The two chairs, he determined judi-
ciously, were ugly. His eyes returned to the ormolu

clock on the chest of drawers. Six-twenty. Morning or evening? It hurt to even think about it.

After he had raised himself gingerly on an elbow to look out the window he felt a bit better and thought he might possibly be able to stand. This proved to be an over-optimistic judgment, and he groaned and lay down again for a while. When the clock had reached six-fifty he made another valiant effort to rise and was this time successful. It had until this moment escaped his blurred attention that he was unclothed and his garments were nowhere to be seen. He wove a path to the tallboy, his face now grimly set. This piece of furniture was entirely empty but for a scrap of lemon-colored ribbon at the bottom.

Face it, Andrew, he urged himself sourly, not only are your clothes not here, but Celeste's are not, either. The baggage! Adding insult to injury. A splash of water from the hand basin helped to revive him somewhat, and he began an exhaustive search of the small house. There was not a single personal item left in the place. It was furnished, at least to the best of his recollection, in the manner in which it had been when let. Perhaps he should be grateful that Celeste had not made off with Mrs. Harrow's old but genteel furnishings.

Having completed this tour of inspection Winterton next surveyed the scene in Small Street and decided that it must be morning rather than evening. He returned to the fourposter and hauled off a sheet which he draped rather artistically about himself. After attempting for some time to summon a street urchin to carry a message for him to the inn he was less amused by the situation than he had been previously. There was not a ha'penny to be found in the entire dwelling, and no self-respecting urchin was willing to take the chance of future reward from the unshaven, queerly dressed man at the window in Small Street.

Winterton wandered disconsolately into the kitchen and found a stale piece of bread to break his fast. He considered the possibilities of emerging into the streets dressed in a sheet and realized at last that Celeste had had her revenge *par excellence*. She had known that he was tiring of her company, that the house was let for only a three-month period, which was drawing to a close. He never let a house for a mistress for a longer period, of course, as he was well aware of his own boredom after even shorter periods of time than that. Thomas had hinted to him, he now recalled, that it might not be wise to be so specific in his arrangements with his mistresses, but Winterton's pride dictated that he have everything understood perfectly. It was the way he indicated he was in charge, he thought ruefully with a sigh. So now Celeste was off with his clothes, his purse (it could not have contained less than a hundred and fifty pounds) and all of her own belongings. He shrugged mentally; perhaps the loss of the money was less distressing than the scene Celeste might have made had he informed her that their liaison was finished.

There was no profit in these thoughts, and Winterton returned to the front window, which would have been better for a cleaning and some new curtains. He renewed his attempts to find a messenger boy, but they were unsuccessful. Eventually someone would come along who knew him and he would be rescued. Patience was not his long suit, but he settled down in a chair by the window, arranged his sheet about him, and watched the passersby.

* * *

Ralph had mixed emotions on arriving at the Hall after his stay with Winterton. He felt desolated at his rejection by Charity, and yet he wanted to see her. He feared she would be embarrassed to be in the same house with him after his unwanted offer. Perhaps Kate could persuade her to stay so that he might at least be near her for a while longer.

Charity was on hand, as was the rest of the family, when Mr. Montgomery drove up with his son. Ralph limped slightly as he entered the house, waving off Susan, who attempted to fling herself on him. He gruffly informed them that he was feeling "quite all right."

"I thought you might like to go to the back parlor," Kate suggested kindly. Her mother exclaimed immediately that he should be in bed.

Ralph tucked Kate's hand under his uninjured arm and said gratefully, "The back parlor will be perfect." He smiled tentatively at Charity, who responded with the tiniest of smiles which did not reach her sad eyes.

"I have brought all manner of books, games, and cards here so they will be within reach," Kate assured him, as Susan solicitously draped a blanket over her brother's knees. "It is only for you to decide whether to expel us or have us entertain you."

Ralph made an effort to keep his eyes from the red-gold hair and the downturned face of his beloved, but he could not choose to send them away. "Let's play whist for penny points, or even for nothing," he offered generously.

"Now this is a change indeed, dear brother," Kate laughed. "Have you lost your taste for gambling?"

"Let it be for imaginary stakes," Charity surprised them by suggesting. "I have always wanted to win a vast sum of money at whist."

Ralph smiled fondly at her and said, "Pound points it is, then. But who is to say you shall win?"

"You'll see," Charity retorted. And they did. She was a remarkably fine player with an excellent memory, putting them all to shame.

The interlude helped put Ralph and Charity at ease with one another, as did the arrival of Benjamin Karst after luncheon. The young people spent an enjoyable afternoon playing cards, talking, and listening to Kate play "Greensleeves" on the dulcimer. While Ralph and Benjamin discussed the farm they now owned, Kate gave Charity an impromptu lesson on the ancient instrument in a far corner of the room. Even as Ralph spoke with his friend, he was constantly aware of the late winter sunlight playing over Charity's hair and features, aware of her gentle voice and the occasional melody of her laugh.

Kate caught the expression on her brother's face as he watched Charity. She had never seen that tender, adoring look on his countenance before. It made her ache for him and long to help him, but she refused to break her word to Charity. They would have to sort it out themselves, and no doubt they would do a better job of it than she could.

The whole family joined for an evening of music and conversation. Benjamin had proposed that afternoon that if Ralph was equal to it they would drive over to the farm the next day. When the family had begun to head for bed, Ralph drifted over to Kate and Charity.

"Would you like to join Benjamin and me tomorrow? Go to the farm, you know. Want to start getting everything in order," he said awkwardly.

Kate noted that this offer upset Charity, so she replied, "Not tomorrow, Ralph. I plan to take Charity to Bristol to see the sights. We had no time on the day she arrived.''

Charity allowed a wisp of a sigh to escape her, and Ralph nodded sadly. ''Another time, perhaps,'' he urged.

''We'll see,'' his sister replied vaguely, and took her friend's arm, squeezed it encouragingly, and led her off amidst mumbled ''good nights.''

10

When Kate and Charity had wandered down High Street and seen the church of St. Nicholas with its 15th-century crypt and Ste. Mary-le-Port in its picturesque street of gabled houses, they admired the tower of All Saints. They passed the comparatively new Christ Church and Kate led her friend left over Corn Street to see Mr. Wood's Exchange where the merchant life of the city should have blossomed, except that the merchants seemed to prefer to deal in the coffee houses. Her favorite sight was the Norman house in Small Street, so they turned right again and Kate was pointing out this structure with its great Hall built in Transitional style and further added to in the Perpendicular style when she heard her name called.

Surprised, she glanced up and down the street, but saw no one she knew. Her name was called again, and this time she discerned the Earl of Winterton's voice, but she could not see him. Charity, in mute shock, pointed a finger at a house down the road on the opposite side. Kate followed her gesture and could see the shoulders and face of Winterton above faded blue curtains at the window of a small house. He was beckoning to her; even at this distance she could tell he was unshaven and was wearing something strange and white.

"I think, Charity, that we would be wise to ignore him," she grinned, "for he has obviously lost his mind, if not his clothes."

"You surely would not abandon him?"

"No, for I can see that he is in need of help," Kate replied. "But I shall be hard-pressed to keep a straight face." Nonetheless she left her friend and with a suitable gravity approached the small window and inquired politely if she could be of assistance to Lord Winterton.

Winterton, thoroughly exasperated with his wait and cursing his fate that the first acquaintance to stroll down Small Street should be Miss Montgomery, found himself at a loss as to what to say to her. He had expected that he would see some male acquaintance or servant to whom he was known, and was sorely tempted at the sight of Miss Montgomery and her friend to ignore this offering of chance. His first reaction had been a muttered "Oh, hell," his second to withdraw from the window, and his third, which he was beginning to regret, to call to her.

"Yes, you could assist me if you would," he began stiffly. "I find myself without resources and could stand the loan of a pound and some shillings."

"I would be delighted to oblige, sir," Kate responded quickly, dipping into her reticule. She had been considering his plight as he hesitated and noted the sheet about his shoulders with a frantic attempt to maintain her composure. He was a very proud man, excessively so, and she could repay him for all his inequities to her by simply bursting into laughter at this point. She would not allow herself to do so, for he was also a neighbor and had assisted her family. As she handed him the money she warned, "However, if that is to send a messenger, I fear you could be out of luck. There is no saying that the urchin you gave it to would not simply scamper off with it to be seen no more.''

''I can give him some now and promise payment of the rest when his mission is complete,'' he informed her coldly.

''And you might see him again. More like you would not.''

Winterton sighed and a wry grin spread over his lips. ''I know you are right, Miss Montgomery, but the alternative is to send you to Thomas yourself.''

''I realize that, sir, and since I consider it the only wise course of action, I am putting myself at your service,'' Kate responded gently.

Charity had hung back from this encounter and could not hear what the two were saying to each other, but she now saw his lordship shrug his sheet-covered shoulders. She turned her back to them to hide her amusement.

''Thank you, ma'am. In that case I would have you go to Thomas, and only he, if you please, and tell him to bring to me here some money and some . . .'' Telling this young woman to send his secretary with some clothing for himself was more than mortifying, it was intolerable.

''Have you no standish and pen there? Some paper on which to write? I am like to forget the half of it,'' Kate suggested with lowered eyes.

''Wait a moment, if you will.'' Winterton withdrew from the window, and Kate did not allow herself to look at Charity for fear of losing her composure. It was several minutes before Winterton returned with a scruffy-looking sheet which might easily have been wallpaper. ''Here,'' he said, thrusting it through the window, his black brows lowered in a frown. ''If you will please deliver it personally to Thomas without delay.''

"On one condition," Kate said calmly.

The little vixen, now she's going to humiliate me, he thought with inward rage. Aloud he spoke evenly. "And what is that?"

"That you will not call to thank me for this day's work. It is forgotten as it is done. Are we agreed?"

"Yes, Miss Montgomery, we are agreed." His gaze fell on her serious brown eyes which promised him that the tale would not be spread. He stretched an unclad arm through the window and she gave him her gloved hand which he took in a firm grasp and shook as though she were a man. He retained it a moment, looked her directly in the eye, and said, "I shall thank you now, then. I am in your debt."

"Not at all. I think Charity was tiring of all my churches and historic buildings." She smiled kindly at him. "You have served my family many a good turn, and I am grateful to have the opportunity to reciprocate. Good day, Lord Winterton."

"Good day, Miss Montgomery." He watched her link arms with Charity and walk purposefully down the road. Perhaps I have misjudged her, he thought, but he was not quite convinced.

Kate spoke not a word to her companion until they were out of Small Street. "I would not for the world have laughed at him," she gurgled, "but I think I have never in my life seen anything so amusing," and she broke into gales of laughter, in which her friend joined unrestrainedly. When they had wiped their streaming eyes and the last of the giggles had been suppressed, they finally walked on toward the stables where the cabriolet and horse were housed. "I know I need not ask you not to breathe a word of this, Charity. I would not have him brought down as the butt of such a joke.''

Charity turned to her friend and laid a hand on her arm. ''You were truly kind to him, Kate, and I know he is a thorn in your flesh. I hope he is appreciative.''

''Goodness, your praise is too generous. My family owes him much, and this was a splendid opportunity to repay him. Perhaps he will show me less animosity in the future. On the other hand, he may be worse for having been put in such a position before me. I am sure even the noble Earl of Winterton was suffering from acute embarrassment, and one cannot blame him. That sheet!'' She was forced to stop again for a moment until she could suppress her laughter.

Although all this merriment slowed their progress somewhat in town, once they were out of Bristol, Kate sprang the horse a bit, saying she did not wish Winterton's discomfort to last longer than necessary. When they reached Winter Manor, Kate stepped down and left Charity in possession of the reins while she approached the house. She was familiar with the elderly butler and greeted him kindly. ''How are you, Manner? Has your rheumatism been acting up?''

''I have been right fine, Miss Montgomery. Pleased that spring is coming on, though.''

''I wonder if I might beg a word with Mr. Single.''

''Certainly. I shall send him to you in the White Parlor,'' he offered as he ushered her into that elegant salon.

Thomas Single was not overly concerned that Winterton had not returned the night before. It would not be the first time he had driven off to Bristol one morning not to return until the next. But the afternoon was advancing by now and he was, if not worried, at least rather surprised, especially since his employer's interest in the young woman in Small Street had certainly seemed to be on the wane. Thomas had not, for instance, been instructed to renew the lease for the house.

When Manner announced that Miss Montgomery awaited him in the White Parlor he gave no indication that this was in any way exceptional, though they were both aware that it was. He proceeded to the parlor and greeted her warmly, for they had known each other for years.

"I shall not keep you in suspense, Mr. Single," Kate began, "for I know you must be perplexed to find me here. I come to bring you a note from Lord Winterton which he directed that I put into your hands alone. I shall not detain you, for it is a most urgent matter. Charity is waiting in the carriage. Good day."

"Good day, Miss Montgomery," he replied, as he held the door open for her and left her in Manner's hands. He turned back into the room and unfolded the disreputable note. Alone, he did not refuse himself the luxury of a good laugh, but he had a genuine regard and affection for his employer and set hastily about collecting the money, clothing, shaving tackle, and food requested in the note. He was able to release the Earl from his particular bondage within the hour.

"For having seen me in the most ludicrous situation of my life," Winterton declared to his secretary as they approached the Manor, "my rescuers have acted with admirable restraint. I expected such consideration of you, Thomas, but certainly not of Miss Montgomery."

"You have never held the young woman in the highest regard, sir, though for my part I think she is deserving of it."

"She accepted a legacy—a very handsome legacy, I

might add—from my brother although she had refused to marry him.''

"It was Carl who made the legacy, sir, and there are few who would have refused it.''

"She should have,'' Winterton retorted stubbornly, and lapsed into silence.

The Earl and his secretary did not pursue the subject further, and each kept an ear open for possible rumors of the former's adventure, but there were none. Miss Montgomery had been as good as her word.

Kate had other matters to concern her. Now that March was here, it was time for Susan to prepare for her London season in earnest. Charity threw herself into these activities for the final days of her stay. She avoided Ralph when possible and was kind but diffident when in his presence. Kate determined to keep them all busy with shopping expeditions, rides, and drives about the neighborhood.

Ralph came to Kate one morning after breakfast, agitatedly pulling his gloves through his hands. "I know you refuse to take a part in my . . . endeavors, Kate, but I cannot bear for her to go without seeing the farm. Promise you I shall not upset her or importune her. I just want her to view the land and the horses we're starting with. Would you support me if I suggested a drive there later?''

His beseeching eyes brought an immediate response. "Certainly, Ralph. Just do not try to be alone with her, for she does not seem to wish that.''

"Thank you, Kate. I promise I'll be the perfect gentleman.''

Kate was aware of Charity's hesitation when the matter was raised.

"I must do some packing, for I shall be leaving early tomorrow," Charity responded quickly.

"I know, my love, but I shall help you immediately when we come back. I long to see the farm again, and I do not wish to part with you on our last afternoon together. Do say you will come."

"Why, of course, Kate, if you wish it," Charity agreed softly.

Kate took her arm and chatted easily of all manner of entertaining things while they prepared for the drive. They rode over in a closed carriage but emerged into warm spring sunlight and walked about the place while Ralph pointed out the pertinent features and asked Kate's advice on various matters. Kate was delighted to see that the countryside was beginning to respond to the spring weather, buds were poking out, and the last of the snow had melted from the wooded areas. Improvements were already starting on the stable, and the horses chosen were admirable beasts. Ralph spoke more knowledgeably about the raising of crops and was, in fact, unable to disguise his love of the place.

Benjamin rode up midway through their tour and called, "Well, Kate, what do you think of it? We've found an excellent tenant, too. And aren't the horses splendid?"

"A very promising start. I envy you. Is the stream the boundary of the property?"

"Yes, Winterton's land is on the other side," Ralph said, pointing westward. "Stream's quite deep in some places, and in the summer the trees on the banks will provide shade. Nice spot for a picnic," he suggested, and could not keep from glancing at Charity.

"Are there fish in the stream?" she asked to divert his attention.

"Tons of 'em," Benjamin laughed. "Well, enough to give a little sport."

They wandered on, Benjamin with Kate and Ralph with Charity. Benjamin was full of plans and dug his booted toe into the earth to show Kate how rich it was. He reached down to crumble it through his bare hands. She pretended dismay at the soiling of his hands, and shock at his wiping them on his pale buckskins. He protested he was no town beau to worry about such things. Their banter effectively covered the conversation of the couple ahead of them.

"Will you be staying long in Bath with your mother?" Ralph asked after a long silence.

"Just for another week. Mama is anxious now to get home, as she misses Papa."

"You live in Daventry all year? You don't go to London ever?"

"Not as a rule. I've been there several times with Papa, and once with Mama, too."

"I was thinking of going to London for a while during the season since Susan is to have her come-out."

"Have you been there often?"

"Enough. Can't say I'd be much help to Susan, though. All my friends there are clothheads like me," he said despondently.

Charity laughed. "You should not be so ridiculous. You are nothing of the sort, and you must know it." She stopped speaking abruptly.

Ralph's eyes showed a flash of hope. "I thought perhaps . . ." He could not miss the alarm which distorted her oval face. "No matter. You know my Aunt Eleanor well, I believe."

"Yes, she is a neighbor and is a great help to Papa in the parish. You have not as yet met Mr. Hall, have you? I think you will like him."

By now Kate and Benjamin had caught up with them, and Charity was grateful that she no longer was required to put Ralph off or change subjects when he pursued avenues she must not discuss. She could not bear to see the look of disappointment that crossed his countenance nor observe the dejected slope of his shoulders as he read the unspoken rejection lying beneath the surface of her tactful words.

11

Kate felt a decided depression of spirits as she waved to Charity until the stagecoach was out of sight. She knew that Ralph had wanted to come to see Charity off, but Kate had refused him, and she felt guilty when confronted with his bleak, unhappy expression. Her friend's visit had managed to divert Kate's mind from consideration of the future, which must now concern her. She had spent several happy years with her aunt and had returned to her family willingly to share in their interests. But Susan was off to London soon, and Ralph was sure to throw himself into the farm. Mr. Montgomery was so pleased with Ralph's newly-found interest in farming and the estates that he spent less time with his daughter and inadvertently cut her off from her source of enjoyment in the land. There were still visits to sick or injured tenants, but they hardly occupied the whole of her time. Mrs. Montgomery was thoroughly wrapped up in Susan's debut, as could only be expected; and though she left Kate to run the house, once Kate had set things to rights, there was really not so much to do there, either.

The occupation of sewing and embroidering, as a full-time pursuit bored Kate. She loved playing the piano-forte and the dulcimer, but they were relaxations for her and she had no serious intent with them.

She had enjoyed her travels most of all and had kept journals of her impressions and experiences. Aunt Eleanor's drawings had provided illustrations, and they had sometimes half-jokingly, half-seriously considered the possibility of putting a book together. But Aunt Eleanor's marriage had halted those thoughts, and Kate did not wish to revive them at this point. Her aunt was like to be far too occupied to even remember them.

Kate had almost, but not quite, been able to tell her father that she dreamed of purchasing the Drew farm for herself. She realized he would be only slightly less shocked than everyone else if she were to do such an outrageous thing. Yet she had the capital and the enthusiasm to engage profitably in such an enterprise. But it would be an embarrassment to her family, and she shrank from so ungrateful an action.

There was very little for a gentlewoman to do, she thought ruefully, except get married and raise a brood of children and manage a household. Would that be satisfying? Would I feel I had accomplished something? I guess one cannot know until one has tried it, she thought. But even marriage looked less likely than ever before. No suitor had thus far really roused her interest, much less touched her heart.

Mr. Montgomery had persuaded her to journey to London with the rest of the family. She had consented only on the understanding that she would return when he did, leaving Susan to have her season unmarred by an aging spinster sister. The trip would provide an entertaining week or two, but it would not solve the dilemma she was trying to solve now. She wanted to do something interesting, rewarding, useful.

Immersed in her thoughts, she led the maid Betsy in and out of shops as she executed commissions for her mother, sister, and brother. These errands took no thought or energy; they were a dull routine. She decided to purchase Ralph something to cheer him, and strolled into a print shop. It might be fun, she thought, to own such a shop. She surveyed the counter and walls strewn with black-and-white and colored prints, inspected the window front, and wondered about the quarters behind the shop.

"Thinking of buying it, Miss Montgomery?"

Startled, she turned to face Winterton and blushed slightly. "Actually, I *was* thinking something like that. I was wondering what it would be like to own such a place. But it is nonsense, of course. Idle speculation."

"You could *afford* to do so, of course, but I doubt that your family would approve, ma'am."

"It seems to me, sir, that there is very little one *can* do to any purpose of which one's family or friends would approve."

"Marriage is the only suitable course for young women," he retorted.

"Well, you know, that seems a very limited prospect to me." Taunted by his exaggerated expression of shock, she continued coldly, but with a blush, "Mary Wollstonecraft called it legal prostitution. Not a very tempting prospect at all."

Winterton narrowed his eyes. "I doubt your parents would approve of your reading Wollstonecraft, either, Miss Montgomery."

"Do you think you should tell them, Lord Winterton? For my own good, of course."

"You are being insolent."

"And you are being patronizing. I am three and twenty and quite capable of deciding what I shall read."

"I doubt most women are capable of an intelligent choice of reading material."

"I assure you your opinion is of not the slightest interest to me. If you will excuse me, I have changed my mind and shall not purchase a print today." Kate wheeled and headed for the door with skirts swishing in an angry hiss.

"Miss Montgomery, a moment," Winterton ordered, but Kate ignored him and slammed the door behind her. His lengthy strides overtook her before she was two doors away, Betsy trudging in her furious wake. He took Kate's elbow in a firm grasp and rasped, "I asked you to stay a moment."

Kate attempted to shake off his hand, but he retained a tight hold. "You did not ask me; you commanded me. I am not one of your wards to calmly accept a raking down from you."

"It has but just occurred to me that I have never repaid the loan you made me," he explained calmly, digging in his pocket.

"Well, be sure to pay me in the streets, your lordship, where it cannot possibly be misconstrued," she snapped and, giving a final shake to her elbow, easily dislodged his hand in his surprise. She once again proceeded on her way, Betsy bewildered and alarmed beside her.

"Oh, ma'am, how you did speak to him," the maid said, awed.

"And so would you were someone so rude to you," Kate laughed. She had more than once heard Betsy tell the youngest footman to mind his tongue.

"But the Earl of Winterton, ma'am," Betsy protested.

"He is no different from other men, Betsy, and—"

"Now that is very true," the judicious voice on her other side said.

"Lord Winterton, I am sure I have made it clear

that I do not desire your company. However, should you wish me to spell it out, I shall.''

"Miss Montgomery, I am sure you would be the first to insist that I run by no inclination but my own. However, I wish to apologize for my rudeness.''

"I don't want your apology, sir.''

"Miss Martin-Smith would not approve of such behavior,'' he responded, his bland expression fixed on her face.

Kate flushed, cast her eyes down, and said sweetly, "But my friend Charity has not spent such a great deal of time being taunted by you, my lord.''

"No, indeed. I'm sure no one has ever had the least desire to taunt her,'' he agreed.

"I'm sorry she has left,'' Kate said suddenly. "It is not only Ralph's disposition she keeps on an even keel.''

"No wonder you are in the mopes,'' he declared, enlightened. "Ralph has his farm, Miss Susan is going to London, and you are at loose ends.''

"How well you put it, Lord Winterton. I am a great admirer of such needle-witted brevity. Perhaps you also prescribe for the 'mopes.' ''

"In your case I could.'' He watched her face set stubbornly, and continued in a more kindly manner. "There is a project here in Bristol I should like you to see. I think it would fascinate you. Is your maid enough of a chaperone to play propriety for us if I take you to a rougher side of town?''

Kate looked uncertain. "What is the project?''

"I would rather show you than tell you. Will you come?'' He regarded her challengingly now.

"Very well. But you must agree to turn back at any time if I ask it.''

"Certainly.'' He offered her his arm, which she took

after a brief hesitation. As they walked along, Betsy reluctantly accompanying them, Winterton began to tell her of the poorer side of Bristol. He vividly described the lives of the destitute and the hopelessness of their future. As they progressed into a section of the town she was not familiar with, he began to point out the signs of decay and neglect, and ragged urchins importuning them for money spoke for themselves.

"You understand, Miss Montgomery, that the long-term relief of this situation is not charity." He supplied some short-term relief to several of the urchins as he spoke. "Over the years the situation of these children can only be improved by preparing them to earn a living which will support them. You know of Hannah More?"

"I have read a number of her works."

"Miss More and her sisters assisted William Wilberforce in starting a school for girls. He was shocked by the poverty and lawlessness of Cheddar and the Mendips. The sisters taught their students spinning, knitting, and the catechism. Miss More's ideas on education for these girls are limited to preparing them to work as servants and inculcating Christian principles. Quite admirable as far as it goes. She is a remarkable woman who must be nearing seventy by now, and she still superintends numerous schools and charities. She has no time for Mary Wollstonecraft's diatribes on female rights, by the way."

"Then she must be lacking in foresight," Kate retorted.

"Be that as it may, she has devoted a great part of her life to *doing* something for women, which Wollstonecraft did not. In fact, considering Godwin's description of her, I would say she did quite the reverse."

"I do not have to approve of her life to be in sympathy with her thoughts on women's rights. In fact, hers was not a particularly well-written book, but in the long run someone must consider the status of women. It is all very well for those of us who have families and money to rely upon them for support, but the plight of those without is pathetic.''

''I understand it was your expression of such a viewpoint that led to the wager my wards took part in,'' he rejoined as he led her toward a building at the end of a dingy street.

Kate stopped abruptly and glared at him. ''And it did not occur to you that such a wager merely serves to illustrate a woman's pathetic situation?''

''Only yours,'' he replied incautiously.

''We will turn back now, Lord Winterton,'' Kate instructed, her face grown pale with mortification. She dropped his elegantly clad arm and linked hers with Betsy's.

Exasperated, Winterton spoke sharply. ''You are intent on misunderstanding me, Miss Montgomery. I admit that was carelessly spoken. What I meant was that few women are prepared to take on an equality with men. You are one who probably could.'' He was talking to her back now and could not judge the response to this speech. There was a long silence; the cries of the street intervened.

At length Kate spoke almost inaudibly. ''The fact that they are *not* prepared does not necessitate that they could not *be* prepared.''

''It remains to be seen. Are you an ardent advocate of female rights, Miss Montgomery?''

''No, but I cannot bear to see women being treated like cattle,'' Kate choked, her back still to him.

''Then come with me, and I will show you how to improve the situation. Ignorance is at the base of it.''

"Where are you taking me?" she asked quietly as she turned to face him.

Winterton was struck forcefully by the lone tear-streak on her face. He was impatient of female hysterics, but there was nothing but dignity writ upon her countenance. Confound the woman, he fumed within himself. "I am taking you to a school where these street urchins you see about you can be taught a trade. Those who are capable and express an interest are also taught to read, something Hannah More would deplore, I fear, as her interest is in stimulating the lower classes to habits of industry and piety, not fanaticism, so she says. My own belief, for what it is worth, is that although the ability to read will broaden the possibilities of employment for the wretched children, it is hardly likely to inspire visions of grandeur. The enclosure laws have driven many from the land to the cities where they will try to find employment in trade. If they can read, they have a better chance to do so."

"Take me to your school." Kate sighed with resignation and accepted his proffered arm once more.

Winterton's manner seemed softer and more enthusiastic once they were in the school and being greeted by Mr. Collins, the headmaster, who asked after Thomas Single. Winterton explained that he had hired Thomas away from the school when they had been able to find a replacement for him. The building which housed the school was older and not very large, but it was kept clean. There were several classrooms and a dining room. Kate was introduced to the two teachers, a woman of middle age and a young man. The school's program was explained to her, with Winterton filling in the details of materials needed.

"You see, there is little reading material which is suitable for our purposes. Hannah More's writings for her schoolchildren are largely religious indoctrination. If we want the children to learn to read, the subject must be something which will interest them. It should relate to the lives they lead or could lead, incorporating simple lessons on economy and honesty and such.'' Winterton stopped to wave out the window at the dirt yard. ''They will do better morally if they have food in their stomachs and a roof over their heads.''

When they had thanked Mr. Collins for the tour and stepped out into the sunlight once again, Kate did not know quite what to say to Winterton. They walked for some time without speaking, Betsy once again following. Kate was considering the various aspects which presented themselves to her. Winterton had just shown her a useful project, as he had hinted he would. The school fascinated her, and she was willing to help support it. Her legacy from Carl made it possible for her to interest herself in such endeavors without involving her family if she wished. Perhaps Winterton hoped she would give away the entire legacy and be done with it! No, he had described her as being at loose ends; therefore he must imagine that she would involve herself actively in the work, which was what most appealed to her in any case. But she could not journey to Bristol very often; it would have to be something she could do at home.

''Why do you think I could write books for them?'' she asked abruptly.

''I don't know,'' he replied frankly. ''I suppose because of the interest you take in farming and your consideration of that print shop this morning. You are not afraid to undertake a project outside a woman's usual scope. Don't you think you could write books for the school?''

''I would like to try. I was thinking just this morning

about the fantasy Aunt Eleanor and I used to have of writing a book on our travels. How would I go about it? I cannot think I would know where to start."

"Talk to Thomas. He still involves himself with the school and knows more about it and its needs than I do. I will agree to spare him three hours a week to come to the Hall to work with you if you think that will help."

"Tomorrow?"

Winterton laughed. "Yes, Miss Montgomery. I shall send him at one."

They had arrived at the inn where her carriage had been left. Winterton offered to take her in to luncheon before she drove home, but Kate protested that they had been gone far longer than expected already. She impulsively put out her hand, and he took it in a firm clasp. "Thank you, Lord Winterton. I . . . well . . . thank you."

12

Kate spoke with her father about her meeting with the Earl and her interest in the school. He was rather puzzled by this enthusiasm on her part, but saw no harm in it. He himself had contributed to the school in the past on Winterton's suggestion, but had never had any interest in seeing the place.

Thomas Single arrived promptly the next day at one, dressed in his usual quiet style, with an earnest face and twinkling eyes. Kate had instructed that he be shown into the back parlor. As they shook hands he remarked, "I hear Lord Winterton has interested you in one of his hobbies."

"Is it one of his hobbies? He said you might be able to direct me if I tried to write some books for the children. Do you think I could? Would it be imposing on you to ask for your help?"

Kate seated herself at the fine, inlaid writing desk and had Thomas take a comfortable chair near her. He had the facility of looking at ease and ready to be of service at the same time. "Yes, I would not be surprised if you could write for the children. Lord Winterton has a knack for recognizing appropriate talents for the school."

"I understand you were a teacher there and that you

still take an interest in it. I cannot imagine where to start on such a project,'' Kate admitted.

''I have been thinking about that since he mentioned it to me. You already have some knowledge of the workings of the countryside. Perhaps a simple tale on the life of a child on a farm—where he lives, what he eats, his observations on the changing of the seasons and the crops, the various jobs he does and sees his parents doing. Something like that.''

''Hm, yes, I should like to work on that. But most of the children are town-bred. Would it be more helpful to write something they would be familiar with?''

''We need that, to be sure. First, though, I would start with something you know best. Then you might work on the town life—again where a child lives and what his parents do, and a description of the work that is done in various shops—the confectioners, grocers, carpenters, basketmakers, drapers, chandlers.''

''I would need help with that, you know. I have not the first idea how a basket is made,'' she admitted.

''Lord Winterton knows I like working on pursuits for the school and has allowed that I may spend several hours a week helping you. That is, if you should like that . . .'' He looked at her inquiringly.

''I shall need your help if I am to do it. Tell me, Mr. Single, how simple should the texts be?''

Kate and Thomas Single spent the next hour considering various questions with regard to the writing, printing, and use of the books before he prepared to leave, promising to provide information she would need. Before he left he handed her a small leather purse with a grin and said, ''Lord Winterton hoped this would be private enough for the return of your loan.''

''Tell him I am duly impressed with his discretion.''

Kate laughed and handed back the purse after removing the money.

Thomas refused this, saying, "You are to keep the purse. It is by way of interest, you understand."

Kate surveyed the purse, a gold-tooled leather pouch with drawstrings. "Very handsome interest his lordship pays." She hesitated over accepting it.

"It is the only way he could thank you. It was his mother's," Thomas explained.

Kate fingered the delicate pouch, nodded, and said, "Thank him for me, Mr. Single, and thank you for your help."

"It was my pleasure, Miss Montgomery."

Kate put the leather pouch away carefully in the dressing table in her room and returned to the back parlor. She made notes for herself and gave considerable thought to the simplest manner in which to present country life to the town-bred children. Her work on the book became interspersed with efforts to assist Susan in preparing her wardrobe for the trip to London and organizing for her own shorter stay there. In fact it was necessary to arrange for the whole family in some matters, as they did not travel often. She had three weeks in which to accomplish this, so there was time for all of her endeavors, including the impending visit of her aunt with her new husband.

Mr. and Mrs. Hall arrived only a few days after Kate had begun to work on the book and there were few people she would rather have set it aside for. The Halls planned a week-long stay, and Kate quietly assumed the extra duties in the management of the household. Her mother was pleased to see her sister and anxious to become acquainted with Mr. Hall.

"Are you as fond of travel as my sister, Mr. Hall?"

she asked as they sat around the tea tray on the afternoon of the visitors' arrival.

"Indeed, yes. It was in Dublin that I met Eleanor and Kate, though I live in Daventry. Have for many years. We had mutual friends in the O'Rourkes. Quite a clan of them there are, too. I know I counted twenty-three gathered under the same roof one afternoon."

"That reminds me, Kate," Aunt Eleanor interjected. "Did I write you that young Patrick is with the Foreign Office now in London? We saw him on our way through and urged him to call on you, Susan, when you are in town. Are you going, too, Kate?"

"Only for a week or so until Mama and Susan are settled. Ralph expects to stay for a while, too, but Papa and I shall return shortly."

"Tell me about Patrick O'Rourke," Susan begged.

"He is the funniest man I have ever met," Kate laughed. "He is forever dreaming up the most crack-brained tales, strewn with gremlins or leprechauns or some such thing, which he will cheerfully swear are the truth."

"And I assure you, Kate," Aunt Eleanor said, "that the seriousness of his post has not in the least diminished that penchant of his. I think they have chosen very well in that young man," she remarked thoughtfully.

"Well, I hope to see him while I'm there," Kate remarked. "I'm sure he will amuse you, Susan, for he is the greatest flatterer. He is not very tall but moves with the most incredible speed, so he is forever surprising one by being where he is not expected."

Mr. Hall nodded. "You can be standing in a group with him when someone announces the intention to leave, and before another of the party has even thought to move toward the door, he is there smiling and bow-ing the fellow out. It came to be a pastime among us to keep an eye on him to see how he managed it.''

Susan was intrigued with the possibilities for sport provided by the young man and vowed she looked forward to meeting him. She must remember to alert her friend Laura to such a good game before ever they met him.

When Kate and her aunt were alone after a while, Kate settled them in the back parlor for a real chat. They were not much closer in age than Kate and her mother, but their years together had put them on a more sisterly footing.

''How is it with you, Aunt Eleanor? Mama has been worried that you would find it a nuisance to remarry at your age and have to accommodate a new husband,'' Kate grinned.

''I have never enjoyed myself more. Your mama! But then, she is so accustomed to life here that she cannot imagine rearranging everything. It goes hand in glove with the love of travelling. You and I must be lost souls indeed in her eyes!''

''She would never say so. But I am sure it gives her a great deal of pleasure to see me safe at home and leading the quiet country life.'' Kate made a slight grimace.

''I have spoiled you, my love. Is it so bad to be here?''

''No, no, not at all. I am very fond of my family. Charity came to stay for some weeks while her mother was in Bath. It was a treat to have her here, for there are not many women my age in the area. I am considered quite the ape leader, I assure you.''

''Do not say so, Kate!'' her aunt retorted with concern. ''I am sure you could have had many offers had you been the least bit encouraging.''

"Why, Aunt, indeed, I have had five since I returned," Kate informed her and proceeded to tell the tale of the spurious suitors.

"What a batch of beef-brains!" Her aunt's eyes sparkled mischievously. "I imagine you have had something to say to the young men."

"I didn't pursue a course of action for a while," Kate sighed, twisting her locket pensively, "but something happened."

"Something you can tell me about?"

"I have been debating that, my dear. I think I must tell you, for perhaps you can solve the problem where I cannot." The locket fell off in her hand and she placed it absently on the mahogany end table, aligning it with the inlaid design. "Ralph fell in love with Charity while she was here. He asked her to marry him, but she refused him. *I* should be able to accept that, I know, but I cannot for the life of me rid myself of the idea that she loves him, too. And that I cannot understand at all," Kate finished sadly.

"And she did not confide in you, love?"

"No. When the subject first came up, she begged me not to meddle, and I promised that I would not. I have never found it so difficult to keep a promise, Aunt Eleanor!" Kate exclaimed wretchedly.

"She gave you no hint at all?"

"Once she said, and I could not credit it, that she did not wish me to pity her."

"I see." Aunt Eleanor sat lost in thought for some time before speaking. "Before you came to Daventry, Charity had two suitors, at different times, and I have long found it difficult to believe that neither of them offered for her. One of them I felt sure she was fond of, and I could not help but notice her agitation when he no longer paid court to her. Yet I have always be-

lieved that he offered for her and was refused.'' She
shook her head perplexedly. "Perhaps she will speak
to me when I reach home, though if she would not talk
about it with you . . .''

"Poor Ralph is suffering, and I am sure that Charity
is also. I felt so helpless not being able to do a thing.''

"Yes," her aunt smiled wryly, "I can imagine you
did not like it one bit to have your hands tied. Let me
see what I can do, my love. I am very fond of Charity.''

"I know. I leave it to you, but I shall understand if
you can do nothing.''

"Tell me what else you have been doing.''

"When Charity left I felt blue-devilled, but Lord
Winterton took me in hand," Kate replied with a rue-
ful grin.

Her aunt's astonishment was unfeigned. "Carl's
brother? You have made your peace with him?''

"Not a bit of it. He still thinks me a heartless, unprincipled wench, but I did him a service—out of necessity, you understand—and he took pity on me and
has suggested that I write a children's book. He is
involved in a school for poor children in Bristol, and
they have not much suitable reading material. I
gather," she said piously, "that the religious tomes
the urchins are usually set to read do not fully serve
their purposes.''

"No wonder. Have you started work?''

"Yes, and I should like you to see it, but even more,
my dearest aunt, I would beg a few sketches from you
for the book. It's about a child's life on a farm. I know
you are very busy now," she hastened to add.

"When we get to Daventry it will take some time
to sort out the two households, I have no doubt, but

while I am here I can make some sketches. What did
you have in mind?''

Kate and her aunt went over the plans for the book
and the list of sketches Kate had considered. During
the days that followed, Aunt Eleanor's sketchbook was
a constant companion on their trips about the neighborhood and the estate. Ralph proudly escorted them
about his farm, but he could not always exclude the
wistfulness which invaded his talk of the future. Mrs.
Montgomery planned a small dinner party for those
who knew her sister in the area. On the day of this
entertainment Kate accepted the task of arranging the
seating of the guests and found to her chagrin that
Winterton was to be one of the guests.

"Pray tell, Mama, why did you invite him?'' she
exclaimed. "He doesn't know Aunt Eleanor from the
next woman.''

"To be sure, my love, but he extended far greater
hospitality to Ralph,'' her mother explained reasonably.

"I am surprised that he accepted.''

"So am I,'' her mother agreed frankly.

"Well, I shall seat him between Aunt Eleanor and
Lady Romsey. I am sure the two of them will keep
him well entertained.''

"Just as you wish, my dear,'' her mother replied
vaguely.

Mrs. Montgomery was in her element when entertaining. She had a gracious air not in the least marred
by her gossamer-like flight from guest to guest. When
the Earl of Winterton was announced, she showed
genuine pleasure and hastened to introduce him to Mr.
and Mrs. Hall, quite sure he would enjoy their company. However, Susan was just as sure that Lord Norris would enjoy meeting them, and he, ever on the

look-out for advancement of his suit, began a very *mature* conversation with them, and the Earl found himself slightly excluded.

Kate joined him, grinning mischievously. "Your ward seems to be making great progress, sir. You are to be congratulated."

"Am I? And I was just about to say the same to you." Winterton regarded her quizzingly.

"Mr. Single was telling me," she said as she moved down the room with him, "that you have a talent for recognizing abilities for your school. I was wondering if that extended to other matters as well."

"What are you up to now, Miss Montgomery?"

"Nothing you would not approve of, I feel sure, my lord. Why, just the other day you set yourself the task of finding useful employment for one of the idle rich. I had much the same goal in mind," she explained modestly.

Winterton's mouth curved in a good-humored smile as he surveyed the occupants of the room. "Which is it to be this time?"

"I cannot help feeling that the heirs Tolbert and Marsh are destined for national affairs," Kate whispered as she shared her secret with wide-eyed innocence.

The black brows drew together in a frown. "You must be daft," he retorted.

"Do you think so? Charity would give me no definite opinion on the matter, not being well acquainted with the young men. But they take a very lively *interest* in such things, and I can only find that encouraging."

"Do you have the least idea what their politics consist of?"

"No," she admitted, not the least abashed. "Does it matter?"

Winterton regarded her exasperatedly. "Surely you can see that it does."

"Consider this, then," Kate suggested. "They fall into discussions of such matters frequently with each other and with everyone else. These discussions are often lengthy but rarely heated. Do you see what that means? They must be in agreement with the majority of our neighbors," she pronounced triumphantly.

"Your reasoning is impeccable, Miss Montgomery." He gave a mock bow to her and proceeded to flick open an enamelled snuff box and extract a pinch. When this procedure was concluded, he continued thoughtfully, "I dare say it could have been worse. You might have chosen medicine or the law for the two nodcocks."

Kate acknowledged this as tacit approval by enlisting his aid. "I have seated you next to Lady Romsey. You might put a word in her ear."

"You are too kind, ma'am. I take it you are seated next to Mr. Marsh."

Kate grinned at him disarmingly. "Why, yes, I believe I am."

Dinner was announced at that point, so their discussion came to an end. The Earl escorted Mrs. Montgomery into the spacious white and gold room ablaze with the light of a crystal chandelier which accented the luster of the dark wood furniture and the rich Axminster carpet. The richly laid table and side table sparkled in the glow, and Kate surveyed the whole with satisfaction. She was seated between Mr. Hall and Mr. Marsh, her sister between the latter and Lord Norris. The two young men in question were not in attendance, but Kate found that much the best arrangement. She bent her attention first on Mr. Marsh, since her sister was unlikely to do so.

"I understand your family goes to London for the season, Mr. Marsh. Mary and Susan talk of little else these days. Do James and Terence accompany you?"

"So they say," he grunted as he attended to his soup. "Might as well. Confounded dull after hunting season."

"Yes, indeed. And I imagine Terence is anxious to be with people who share his interest in politics," Kate suggested thoughtfully.

"What's that?" the poor man gasped as he attempted to swallow the brimming spoonful of soup he had succeeded in getting to his mouth.

"I was merely thinking that he must be sadly devoid of stimulating political company here in the country. There is nothing to rival the gossip and intrigue of London on that score."

The bewildered Mr. Marsh merely stared at her for a moment, his spoon poised clumsily in his hand. "Young lady, I have not the faintest idea what you are talking about," he finally managed.

Kate in her turn looked perplexed. "Why, we were speaking of your eldest son Terence, sir. And his fascination with politics."

"Who says he's fascinated with politics?"

"He speaks of little else when hunting season is over. Both he and Geoffrey Tolbert have the most admirable interest in the affairs of state. I have often wondered that they do not try for seats in Parliament. It must be exciting to have a hand in those government actions which affect our own lives, do you not agree?"

"Never thought about it," he mumbled over a mouthful of roll.

"But think of the taxes and laws which are enacted!

Think of the money which is spent! Surely these are not matters we wish to have handled by just anyone!''

"Perhaps not," he reluctantly agreed as he speared a morsel of roasted cheese.

"I'm sure my father is most particular about the member from his district," Kate declared majestically, as though her father's honor had been impugned.

"To be sure. Yes, certainly. As I am," he protested while lifting his wineglass recklessly.

"Of course you are," Kate murmured placatingly. "I should imagine it would be a great comfort to have one's own son representing one's interests in Parliament," she said thoughtfully.

As a drop of wine trickled down his chin, Mr. Marsh regarded her curiously and commented, "No doubt."

Feeling that she had pushed the matter as far as she dared, Kate now changed the subject and happened to glance across the table where Winterton was regarding her with amusement. She winked at him, and he choked discreetly on his baked trout. Kate returned her attention to her other neighbor.

Kate's Aunt Eleanor did not miss this interchange; there was very little that escaped her attention. She set herself to get acquainted with Lord Winterton. "I believe I knew your parents many years ago. Not very well, you understand. But it was through your mother that I was introduced to Sir John, my first husband. He was a friend of the Countess's oldest brother."

"That would be my Uncle Septimus Conway, ma'am?"

"Yes. Is he still alive?"

"Very much so, though he has outlived three wives. He still expects an earthquake any day; he remembers the ones in '50 as a lad of ten," the Earl grinned.

"I fear he will be disappointed," Aunt Eleanor replied.

"No doubt. But I am convinced that it is the expectation which keeps him alive, for he has become quite fanatic on the subject."

"Kate and I met an ancient lady in Ireland who had originally moved there for fear of those London quakes."

"I understand you and your niece have done considerable travelling. It must be rather difficult for two women alone."

"Well, I admit it was easier with Mr. Hall this time, but on the other hand, wherever one goes with Kate, there is an adventure."

"I cannot doubt it," Winterton replied and glanced over at that young woman, who was now in close conversation with her new uncle.

Aunt Eleanor in turn inspected Winterton's rugged features, his black brows and soot-colored wavy hair. When he returned his gaze to hers, his blue eyes still merry and the corners of his mouth twisted, she determined that he was rather attractive when not on his dignity. "Have you done much travelling, Lord Winterton?" she asked politely.

"A little. I spent some months in Italy when I was younger, and I have gone to Ireland several times, but I have been to France only once. I have a strong desire to see Greece one day."

"Kate and I had been contemplating a trip there, but then Mr. Hall and I were married. He and I may go there some day," she mused wistfully, "but we agreed that a shorter trip would serve best at this time. We are faced with the task of combining two households when we return, and I imagine it will be no small matter."

"I wish you well," Winterton smiled and made a mock toast with his wineglass. "I am content to leave all domestic matters to my secretary."

"And I," she grimaced, "left far too many of them to Kate. What I am to do with two butlers, two house-keepers, and half a dozen footmen is beyond me!"

"Perhaps your house could be let with the servants, unless you intend to sell it," Winterton suggested.

She nodded sadly. "I suppose that would be wisest. And I should not regret leaving the house, mind you, but Mr. Hall has such a tartar of a housekeeper that I really cannot believe we shall get on very well to-gether." She sighed and picked abstractedly at her meal. "I'm glad you reminded me of it; I shall discuss it with Kate."

Winterton allowed her to follow her own thoughts and turned to Lady Romsey, who was beginning to feel neglected. However, he chose a subject close to her heart when he did speak to her, so she was inclined to forgive him.

"I have not seen much of Geoffrey recently, Lady Romsey. But I imagine he has been busy. I heard a whisper that he is interested in getting a seat in Parliament."

Lady Romsey was not one to admit there was any-thing about her son that she did not know. She gave herself a moment to consider this intelligence by sip-ping carefully at her wine. Then she said cautiously, "It would be very fitting for him, I think."

"Indeed. He seems to take an interest in the affairs of state, and it cannot be harmful to him to know how to go on one day, in the distant future, of course, when he takes a seat in the Lords."

"As you say," Lady Romsey concurred. Then, feel-ing that she was not showing the proper enthusiasm

about such a worthy project, she continued glibly,
"And I am sure Lord Romsey has sufficient influence
to conclude the matter expeditiously." She beamed
proudly on the Earl for her quick grasp of the situation.

Winterton was hard put not to glance over at Miss
Montgomery, but he restrained himself and replied,
"I have not the least doubt of it."

Lady Romsey was not unrelieved when her attention
was claimed by Ralph at this moment, and she listened
patiently while he told her of his farm. Winterton
thankfully resumed his meal.

After dinner Kate found herself sought out by Winterton when the men joined the ladies. He refused her
offer to join a table of whist-players. "Nor do I wish
to be left at the mercies of Lady Romsey or Mrs.
Marsh. And I hope you will not trot off to play the
pianoforte or act the hostess. This is your mother's
party, and she is apparently enjoying her role, so come
and sit with me for a while." He led her firmly to a
sofa a short distance away from the others and waited
politely while she seated herself. He had never seen
her so modishly dressed, in a blue silk and wool dress
with a richly woven border in dull reds, deep golden
yellows, light and dark greens which became her to
admiration. The short petal sleeves and cross-over
bodice were a distinct change from the long sleeves
and fichus she sported on less formal occasions. If
Winterton had been addressing Celeste he would have
had no trouble turning a compliment, but with Miss
Montgomery he merely said, "You are looking well
this evening."

"How kind of you to say so, Lord Winterton." Kate
repressed a desire to smile and, in his own formal

accents, remarked, "And it is a treat for us to see you in other than buckskins and top boots."

The smile which altered his rugged face appeared. "Thomas assured me they would not do for such an occasion, though I was loath to part with them. Not being beloved of my neighbors, as your father recently informed me, I am not often invited to country dinner parties."

"Surely my father was never so rude! And he had the audacity to criticize Ralph and me! Why, I am sure *I* never told you anything half so unkind." Her indignation was belied by the twinkle in her eyes which met his merrily.

"You underestimate yourself, my dear Miss Montgomery. On numerous occasions you have cut me to the quick."

"No, have I? How splendid! That is, I am sure I never meant to do more than pay you in kind, my lord."

He lifted an admonitory finger. "You have unknowingly taught me a great deal about yourself this evening. I had no idea how easy it was to manipulate people before now."

"That is because you are used to ordering them about, sir," she retorted. "If you were not in a position to do so, you would have learned long ago, I dare say, for I have no illusions about your grasp on your affairs. I take it Lady Romsey took the bait?"

"In one gulp. Were you as successful with Mr. Marsh?"

Kate considered this for a moment as she toyed with her fan. "No, I cannot believe I was. Mr. Marsh was at first incredulous at such a notion, then bewildered as to how to handle it and his meal at the same time, and finally, I think, convinced that I am a trifle wanting upstairs.'' She sighed deeply and snapped the fan shut. ''You see how it is, Lord Winterton. Even in such a small matter your words carry so much more weight than mine. Do you suppose that is because you are a peer, or because I am a woman?''

''Probably both, but I would not let it concern me, if I were you. In the last month you have set into motion a number of projects for which you might be justly proud.'' His eyes locked with hers in a most disconcerting way.

''You . . . don't deplore my methods?''

''I am all admiration of them, Miss Montgomery.''

Kate flushed slightly and lowered her eyes. Impossible as it seemed, he was not mocking her, and his intent gaze made her feel slightly disturbed. ''I try, occasionally, to change, but I cannot resist the temptation to meddle,'' she said with an attempt at lightness.

''No amount of haranguing or bullying seems to work half so well as a few well-placed suggestions with fellows such as your brother or my ward. What did you say to Charles?'' he asked curiously.

''I told him I thought Susan needed to marry a mature man.''

Winterton's shoulders shook with amusement. ''Now, why didn't I think of that? He has become almost oppressive with his maturity, though.''

''Yes, but in time it will sit well on him, I think, don't you?'' she asked anxiously, raising her eyes once more to meet his.

He was struck by the earnestness in them and very nearly reached out to touch her cheek. To cover the half-gesture he had made, he slipped a gold snuff box from his pocket and flicked it open. ''But, of course, Miss Montgomery. He needs only to accustom himself to it.'' Carefully he extracted a pinch of snuff and inhaled it, but he was unable to rid himself of the desire to touch the charming face turned up to him and he was almost relieved when he noticed that Mrs. Montgomery was bearing down on them to extract her daughter from what she thought, mistakenly, must be a most unwelcome tête-à-tête.

13

"My dear, I shall miss you," Aunt Eleanor told Kate as she hugged her before departing. "I shall take your advice about the housekeeper, but heaven knows if it will work for me," she sighed. "I know it would for you. And I shall see what can be done about Charity. I hope you will plan to visit this summer, even if only for a few weeks."

"Let us see how things go on. Thank you for the drawings; I hate to have asked it of you, but you know how I am with such things." Kate grinned.

"I enjoyed it, love. We must think to our travel book one day. I hope your visit to London is pleasant." There were many things she wanted to say, but felt it wiser to keep her own counsel. Mr. Hall handed her into the travelling carriage amidst the general fare-wells of the family, and they departed.

At least this time, Kate thought, I have something to occupy my time. She headed for the back parlor to work on the book, but Susan was having trouble containing her excitement these days and came to sit with her sister.

"You will teach me how to go on, will you not? And where to find the proper clothes? Mama has not been to town for so many years that she is afraid she will not know who is fashionable nowadays. And

Mama will need to have new gowns, too,'' Susan said, eyeing her sister beseechingly.

"Dear Susan, I shall help you in whatever I can, but I have no superior knowledge of London. Aunt Eleanor and I have been through town many times, but I never had to undergo the rigors of a season. Lady Stockton and Laura will teach you how to go on. And I should have thought your wardrobe quite adequate already. We have packed two trunks for you,'' Kate reminded her.

"Oh, Kate, you know those are the merest fripperies. I probably shall not be able to wear the half of them, for Bristol seamstresses are certain to be far behind London in fashion. And Mama insists that I shall not buy a hat until we reach town!''

"From what I have seen in the *Ladies' Magazine* I do not blame her. I am sure you could never find anything so gaudy or impractical in Bristol.''

"And have you anything decent to wear?'' Susan asked with concern.

"My dear sister, you will not be ashamed of me. I shall show you some gowns I got in London last year which have hardly been worn. They are safely packed away for just such a venture.''

The sisters adjourned to Kate's room and Susan was duly impressed with her sister's wardrobe, for it was elegant if small. "I shall only be there a week or so, hardly time enough to wear everything,'' Kate assured her. "But I would ask a favor of you, Susan. Do you think you would have time to look me out a piece of lace for this blue satin? It really needs something about the cuffs, don't you think?''

Susan considered it thoughtfully. "I have just the thing! And I will sew it on for you right now.''

Having thus successfully disposed of her sister for

an hour, Kate returned to the back parlor to work on the children's book, which she had had to put aside for the last week. Her aunt's drawings inspired her to weave a story around the little lad who appeared in many of them, and she felt a sense of satisfaction when she left it for luncheon.

Although the demands were heavy in the last days before their departure, she spent many hours on the book. She was truly disappointed two days before her journey to receive a note from Thomas Single excusing himself from calling because Lord Winterton was ill. "I should come regardless, you understand, but his lordship is such an irascible patient that I fear for the household were I to depart for several hours." Kate could have wept with frustration; she had finished the book and wished to have Mr. Single see it before she left. It had actually been her plan, if he found it acceptable, to take it to London and have it printed while she was there.

"Papa," she began, when she had tracked him down, "would it be all right, do you think, if I drove over to Winter Manor with Betsy? I really should like Mr. Single to see the book before we leave for London and have his comments on it."

"Does he not usually come here?"

"Yes, but Winterton is ill, and Mr. Single refuses to leave the Manor."

"I suppose it will be acceptable. I know you are anxious to be finished before we go to London," he said indulgently.

"Thank you, Papa. I shall drive carefully," she forestalled him.

Spring had taken over the countryside. The lanes were muddy, but the trees sporting their new greenery made up for the splatters. There were even some spring flowers to be seen, their color splashed against the neat farmhouses. Everything looked fresh, and Kate almost regretted leaving the country for town at such a time.

Betsy sat quietly as they rode; then, nerving herself, she asked Kate a question which had been on her mind for some time now. "Do you think, Miss Kate, that I could learn to read?" she asked shyly.

"Why, Betsy, I feel sure you could. It never occurred to me that you did not know how. What a fool I am! Spending all this time writing a book for children to learn to read from and not once considering that there are those on the estate who have never learned! Let me think about it for a while, Betsy." For the remainder of the journey Kate turned the matter over in her mind, and she determined to speak with Mr. Single about it.

Thomas was surprised when Kate was announced, but he directed that she be shown to his office immediately. "I hope you will forgive me for interrupting you at such a time, Mr. Single, but I was anxious that you see the book before I leave for London." She seated herself in the chair he drew up for her and handed him the package. "You will note that my aunt has done some illustrations, which I think are excellent." Kate sat back in her chair and tried not to look anxious while Thomas went through the package carefully. He made several marks as he progressed and finally looked up at her, smiling. "This is exactly what we need, Miss Montgomery. I have changed a few words which would be especially difficult for the children because they are not pronounced as they are spelled. Your aunt's drawings are perfect. And . . ." He was interrupted by a soft tap on the door.

Manner entered soundlessly at Thomas's call and

excused himself for intruding. "His lordship," he announced grimly, "is in immediate need of your services."

Thomas cast his eyes heavenward and begged Miss Montgomery to excuse him for a few moments. "More likely half an hour," he mumbled as he strolled out the door.

However, he returned within ten minutes and seemed somewhat embarrassed. "Lord Winterton has requested that you wait on him in his bedchamber," he said apologetically. "I informed him that I did not think it proper for you to do so, but he insisted there could be no impropriety if I were present. He is past the contagious stage, at least," he offered.

"Contagious stage of what?" Kate asked incredulously.

"I don't think he would appreciate my telling you," Thomas laughed. "He contracted the disease while visiting another of his projects, so it was all in a worthy cause."

When Kate did not offer any objection, Thomas picked up her book and preceded her to the door. "I must warn you," he said with twinkling eyes, "that he is in a foul mood."

"One seldom sees him otherwise," Kate retorted primly and allowed Thomas to lead her up the magnificent staircase.

The room she entered after a considerable walk was nearly the entire width of the west wing of the Manor. Although she was impressed by the size of the room, it paled in comparison with the bed on which Lord Winterton lay. Delicately carved, tapering bedposts supported a japanned cornice which acted as frame for a magnificently domed tester. The dome was surmounted by carved armorial bearings, and four pairs of turtledoves marked the four corners of the tester and served as finials for the bedposts. Valances of blue damask hid the legs and had overdrapings of white tasselled swags. The curtains and tester were of blue damask and the counterpane was white.

"What are you staring at?" Winterton asked irritably.

"I am overcome by your lordship's bed," Kate replied reverently, hoping that her voice would carry the thirty feet from the door to this magnificent structure.

"I should have prepared you," Thomas whispered aside.

Kate shook with mirth as she approached Lord Winterton, and one glance at his face undid her. "You have the measles!" she exclaimed and burst into laughter. Even his steely-eyed glare could not stop her, and she dropped helplessly into a chair Thomas thoughtfully pushed forward.

Winterton assumed his most haughty expression and remarked quietly, "I cannot abide a hysterical female."

"Shall I leave?" Kate inquired, as she rose and wiped her eyes.

"Sit down!" he bellowed. "And control yourself."

"Yes, my lord."

"I have something to say to you."

"Yes, my lord."

"And stop yes-my-lording me," he growled.

"Yes, sir."

"I want you to know that I have sustained a most unwelcome visit from Lord Romsey, all on your account."

"I am sure I never sent him to you. I would have remembered."

"He came, so he informed me, to solicit my support

for his son in the matter of acquiring a seat in Parliament,'' Winterton retorted dauntingly.

"Oh."

"Is that all you can say for yourself?"

"I think we should be quite pleased with the results of our venture," Kate informed him smugly.

"Do you?"

"Of course. If you did not want Geoffrey to run for a seat, you should not have helped me. I did not really thank you for the effort, but I am grateful, and I had no idea you had brought such fine results."

"I should not consider a two-hour visit from a bore like Romsey to be in the nature of a fine result!"

"Did he mention anything about Terence Marsh? Did we make any progress there?" Kate asked, intent on ignoring his heavy sarcasm.

"No," Winterton replied exasperatedly, "he did not mention Marsh."

"Well, one of two is not bad."

Before Winterton could unleash his growing choler, Thomas stepped forward and handed him Kate's book. "I have advised Miss Montgomery that this is exactly what we need. I thought you might care to see it."

Winterton glared once more at Kate before carefully perusing the package. "Who did the drawings?"

"My Aunt Eleanor," Kate said softly.

"They are excellent. And the book will serve," he commented gruffly.

Thomas regarded his employer reproachfully, and Winterton relented. "This book is very good, Miss Montgomery. I shall have the whole printed and it will be in use. . . ."

"No," Kate interrupted.

Winterton looked at her blankly, and Thomas

showed his dismay. *"I* shall have it printed," Kate informed them. "How many will be needed?"

"I have always intended to have it printed," Winterton responded stiffly, while Thomas smiled at her, shrugged, and said, "Twenty will do."

"Excellent. That is settled," Kate replied and rose to leave. "Good Lord!" she exclaimed suddenly, turning to Thomas. "He was not contagious when he was at the Hall for dinner, was he? If anything happens to spoil Susan's season . . ."

"No, no, Miss Montgomery," Thomas soothed her. "It was the day following that he visited the sick ward. I am sure you have nothing to alarm you on that score."

"Thank heaven," Kate breathed with relief. "Oh, and I wanted a word with you on another matter before I leave, Mr. Single, if you might spare a moment."

"I am in need of Mr. Single's services, Miss Montgomery," Winterton informed her coldly.

Kate turned to stare at him. "You should be ashamed of yourself, setting your whole household on its ears for a simple case of the measles," she scoffed. "I'm sure Mr. Single has better things to do than wait upon you."

"But, Miss Montgomery," Thomas interposed, scarlet with embarrassment, "I am employed for just that purpose."

"Stuff! Lord Winterton promised me three hours a week of your time, and I am sure you would be better employed to that purpose than bringing him vinaigrettes and . . . and hot bricks!"

"I have never used a vinaigrette in my life," Winterton rasped.

"Well, I shall send you one to keep you company!" Thomas choked and turned aside to cough quietly,

unable to meet the Earl's blazing eyes. Kate regarded
Winterton intently, her own eyes snapping, until he
burst into laughter. "I should like you to know,
Thomas," he informed his secretary, "that Miss
Montgomery once informed her maid in my hearing
that I am just like any other man."

Kate blushed but said defiantly, "And so you are."

Winterton considered her defiant little chin, her
blushing cheeks, her straight nose, and her steady
brown eyes. No wonder Carl had been so taken with
her, he thought, only to bring himself up sharply. He
was not aware that he spoke aloud when he said,
"Good God, I must be weaker than I thought I was."

Kate thought he was castigating himself for having
no retort for her. Thomas, however, sensed the affect
of Kate's presence on his employer and had a clearer
understanding of the words. We are in for some prime
sport, he thought with the usual twinkle in his eye.
His lordship will hardly allow himself an easy time of
it, after all he has said of her.

Kate was contrite, imagining she had overtired Winterton. "Pardon me, sir. I should not have stayed so
long or been such a nuisance. I hope you feel more
the thing very soon." She made a little curtsy and
headed for the door.

"Do you go to London for the season?" he called
after her, cursing himself for this attempt to delay her.

"No. Just for a week or so to see Susan and Mama
settled," she turned to answer. "I would be grateful
if . . . when you get there . . . You are going, are you
not?"

"Yes. What is it I can do for you?" he asked encouragingly.

"Mama has not been to London for so long, and
there are so many loose screws there. I know Ralph

means to keep an eye out for Susan, but he is . . . not so very happy just now.'' Kate stared disconsolately at the package in her hands and wished she had not begun this request.

''Is it so very difficult to ask a favor of me?'' Winterton queried, a small frown on his brow.

''I cannot think why I should ask you at all,'' Kate replied frankly. ''It is nothing to do with you, of course. I must leave you to rest now.'' She managed to slip out the door Thomas patiently held open before Winterton could speak again.

Once in the corridor Kate followed Thomas in silence the lengthy distance to the stairs before she remembered her need to discuss Betsy's request with him. ''On the way here my maid was asking me about learning to read. Do you think I could teach her?''

''Certainly, Miss Montgomery,'' Thomas responded. ''There is no mystery to teaching. It requires only the desire, knowledge, and a vast quantity of patience.''

''Ah, well, patience is not one of my attributes, as you have seen. But I could try. Do all the servants at Winter Manor know how to read?'' she asked curiously.

''Most of them. Lord Winterton employs children from the school sometimes, and my brother's wife teaches those others who wish to learn.''

''Your brother lives nearby?''

''He has the living at Stasby,'' Thomas explained. ''His wife takes it as her responsibility to do for the minds what my brother attempts to do for the souls. Perhaps you could talk with her when you return from London.''

''I should like that. Thank you, Mr. Single, for all the help you have given me.''

"It has been my pleasure, Miss Montgomery, I assure you. I seldom get the opportunity to hear the Earl scolded." He shook hands with her solemnly and escorted her and Betsy to their waiting carriage. "Enjoy your trip to London."

14

The Montgomerys set out for London with an impressive entourage. Mrs. Montgomery, Kate, and Susan rode in the travelling carriage, followed by Ralph with a groom in the repaired curricle, and Mr. Montgomery mounted on his favorite stallion. A further carriage followed with various servants and luggage piled high and tied on. Bringing up the rear were several grooms who would proceed at a slower pace to bring the Montgomery horses forward when they were changed after the second stage each day. The procession started early on a sunny day in late March, and Susan felt decidedly ill with the excitement, the anticipation, and the swaying of the carriage.

Kate drew forth several guide books from the bundle at her feet and enlisted Susan's help in identifying various landmarks as they progressed. Kate kept up a flow of discourse on her previous travels and their amusing aspects while Susan grew accustomed to the motion. By the time the first change was made at the White Lion in Bath, Susan looked better and Mrs. Montgomery was so familiar with the movement that she was dozing easily.

After luncheon in Pickwick, Mr. Montgomery joined them in the carriage. They passed the hamlet of Cross Keys and climbed Rowden Hill toward Chippenham with its narrow streets and balustraded bridge over the Avon. Kate spent most of the afternoon pointing out the sights and discussing London ways with Susan. They saw the White Horse carved in chalk near Cherhill and the Lansdowne Column; Kate talked of the strange Silbury Hill and the Druid stones at Avebury. Eventually Susan fell asleep, and Kate produced a volume of *Sense and Sensibility* from her bundle and proceeded to read until they began to draw close to Marlborough, where they were to dine and spend the night. Ralph had passed them along the way and had arranged matters at The Castle, and Kate smiled gratefully at him as they went directly to their rooms to refresh themselves before their meal. Although the rest of the family were content to rest quietly before retiring early, Kate urged Ralph to walk about the town with her, for she was desirous of some exercise after a whole day cooped up in the carriage.

It was growing dark, and Kate was intrigued by the lights to the east of town, so she and Ralph directed their steps in that direction. Coming around the spur of the hill at the entrance to town, they were fascinated by the spectacle of a gypsy encampment—white tents, caravans, fires burning, bronzed figures in brightly colored clothes. As Kate began to ascend the steep hill for a closer look, Ralph expostulated, "Don't think you should, Kate. Rather wild-looking people. Haven't a weapon with me."

"Pooh. We shall come to no harm. I would like a closer look, and I'll be bound you would, too," she retorted.

Since he could not deny this obvious truth, they trudged nearer to the encampment and were greeted by an old, wrinkled woman who pressed them to let her tell their fortunes. Ralph was aghast at such a suggestion, but Kate, with glowing eyes, said, "I should like to know what she has to say, Ralph," and seated herself on the offered stool.

The wizened ancient took her hand and studied it, a variety of expressions crossing her countenance. Ralph looked on with amusement and some anxiety but said nothing.

Finally the gypsy spoke, her voice a musical sing-song. "You do not know your heart, but you shall. The past is buried but must be explained. Do not be afraid, for your heart has chosen wisely; your head must be guided by it." She stopped speaking abruptly and honored Kate with a gap-toothed smile.

"Thank you," Kate said, handing the woman a half crown. "I shall consider your words carefully."

As they turned away, Ralph whispered, "I should think you'd have to. Couldn't have meant a thing far as I can see."

Kate's brow puckered in a puzzled frown. "Perhaps not, but I *feel* she spoke directly to me." Kate shrugged her thinly clad shoulders in a gesture of dismissal. "Let's return. Mama will fret if we are long, and we make an early start in the morning."

Ralph dismissed the gypsy from his mind immediately, but Kate tossed in her unfamiliar bed and considered the words thoughtfully. She could put only one interpretation on them, and this she refused to believe. Her cheeks felt hot with embarrassment even at contemplating such a thing. Oh, it is all nonsense, she told herself fiercely. How can I be such a pea-goose? Gypsies! I had as soon consult chicken scratchings. Nevertheless, it was several hours before she slept.

They made an even earlier start the second day, and Kate pointed out the gypsy encampment to Susan as the carriage labored up the steep and badly surfaced

Forest Hill. Even as she spoke, the old gypsy fortune-teller, who was brewing something over an open fire, turned around and gazed directly at her, making a gesture of farewell. Kate returned the gesture with a smile and called Susan's attention to the Savernake Forest of beeches and oaks which massed along the roadside. They had luncheon at the King's Head in Thatcham and pushed on to the Bear at Maidenhead for dinner and the night. Susan had recovered her usual spirits by now and was not disturbed by Kate's unusual silence.

On the third and last day of their journey to town Susan was unable to contain her excitement and Kate indulgently encouraged her, though she did not neglect to point out The Windmill on Salt Hill where the Four-in-Hand Club made their periodic grand parades nor fail to relate the grisly history of the Ostrich in Colnbrook. On the other hand Kate did not urge Ralph to allow her to drive his curricle over one of the stages as she had planned, though she did ride with him for the last few miles to arrive at the house in Brook Street ahead of the rest of the party.

Kate was pleased with the stately dark brick residence they now approached.

The exquisitely detailed wrought-iron fence and the two colonades complemented the square stone lintels and the round and triangular pediments over the full-length windows. The entry was dignified without being overly imposing; the door opened as they arrived. Sampson descended the stairs with proper London gravity to welcome Kate and her brother, informed them that the servants' carriage had arrived these two hours past, having made an earlier start, and that things were in a way to being ordered as quickly as possible.

The calm of the exterior was belied by the bustle

within. Trucks and portmanteaux were being carried hurriedly from the entry hall to various rooms up the grand staircase. Kate wandered from room to room, impressed with how well Lady Stockton had done by them. The furniture was elegant and the décor subdued. It was the perfect atmosphere from which to launch Susan in society. Although the Montgomerys could make no pretentions to the *haut ton*, Lady Stockton was determined that under her patronage Susan should have the entree to all but the very grandest homes.

By the time the remainder of the family arrived, Kate and Butterfield had organized the proper distribution of the luggage, maids were hanging gowns in wardrobes, and footmen were looking to the dispersal of the servants' belongings. The cook had already embarked on preparation of the evening meal, and meanwhile had produced a magnificent tea to revive the travellers.

"Such a delightful house!" Mrs. Montgomery exclaimed. "Not at all the sort of place available to be let in my day. I must write a note to Lady Stockton without delay to thank her." She nibbled a biscuit as she appreciatively ran her eye over the admirable proportions of the drawing room, the marble fireplace, and the delicate plasterwork of the ceiling. Her sigh of contentment brought a grin to Susan's expressive countenance.

"You know, Kate, Mama had rather expected shabby furniture and mice in the floorboards."

"I'm not surprised. It is unnerving to let a house without seeing it," Kate responded. "But we should have known that Lady Stockton would find the best to be had. Shall we walk in the park for a while? It is but a step, and it will give you some ideas for our shopping expedition tomorrow.''

''I should not go out in these rags,'' Susan giggled, ''but I cannot bear to sit here when there is so much to be seen. Give me ten minutes to look out a bonnet and mantelet.''

Their stroll in the park was overwhelming for Susan. Country-bred and never having been to London before, she was quite overcome by the ostentatious costumes sported there and somewhat amused by many of them.

''I know you will wish to be dressed in the first stare,'' Kate informed her, ''but I cannot see you choosing anything pretentious. There is one thing I would mention, though. In our neighborhood you have known all the men since you were born, and you can trust them to behave as they ought. But I beg you will be cautious here in town. There are charming rogues and handsome scapegraces. It is the mode for them to be flattering and well-mannered, and it is not easy to resist such attention.''

''I'm sure I could not,'' Susan sighed.

''Let me tell you a trick I have always used. It is not infallible, but it has helped me more than once. I ask myself, 'Would Papa approve of him?' If the answer is no, it is no difficult matter to ease him off. If I can honestly say that Papa would approve of him, well, then I just enjoy myself, as you will. But you are a very attractive young woman, Susan, and you will have more young men to judge.''

Their discussion was interrupted by the arrival of a curricle driven by a jubilant Lord Norris. ''Famous!'' he cried. ''I did not know you had arrived in town as yet, though I had been wondering how long I must wait to call when you did.'' He jumped down from the curricle when his groom arrived at the horses' heads.

"Charles, how nice it is to see a familiar face,'' Kate greeted him.

Susan smiled shyly when he turned from her sister to take her hand. "We arrived only an hour or so ago, but Kate and I thought a walk in the park would be beneficial. And so it has been,'' she concluded without giving any indication as to whether this approbation referred to the chance of fresh air, the sight of the current fashions, or the fortuitous meeting with Lord Norris himself.

"It must have been a slow and tiring journey with the whole household,'' he commiserated. "How is your house?''

"I think we shall find it quite comfortable,'' Susan replied. "In fact, it is lovely.''

"May I call tomorrow?'' Charles asked, turning his gaze to Kate.

"Of course, but not early, for we shall be shopping a good part of the day. Come for tea late in the afternoon,'' Kate suggested.

"I shall look forward to it. I must not keep the horses standing any longer,'' Charles said, anxiously glancing at the prancing pair. "Give my regards to your parents and Ralph.''

When he had driven off Susan asked softly, "Would Papa approve of him?''

Kate smiled gently and took her sister's hand to press it comfortingly. "Of course he would, goose. But you are both young, and it will do neither of you any harm to make sure of your minds. And to get a little town polish,'' she added with a smile.

Susan said no more as they headed back toward the house, and Kate did not wish to interrupt her thoughts.

Since it would be less than a year before Charles reached his majority, it did not really matter if Winterton approved the match, Kate thought. And, besides, she was probably silly to have thought he would do so in any case.

The first days of their stay flew by in a whirl of shopping, fittings, and making calls upon their acquaintances in the city. Kate immediately attended to the matter of finding a printer for the book and was excited at the prospect of returning home with the finished product. Ralph continued about his business absently, but did not speak to his sister about Charity. He haunted Tattersall's and talked with every knowledgeable man about breeding horses; he drank sparingly and gambled occasionally with his former friends from London. When the entire family attended the theater with Lady Stockton's party, they encountered Patrick O'Rourke.

He made his way with his usual astonishing speed to their box during the first intermission. One moment they noticed him across the way in a box with several other people, and the next he was at the door of their own box, greeting Kate eloquently.

"Miss Montgomery, sure an' I've never seen a lovelier sight! Bewitching! And here have I been just this evening telling the leprechaun I found in my coach that you might come to London. He told me it was highly unlikely, so we made a small wager. I shall be pleased to inform him of my success." The handsome young man grinned engagingly and finally released the hand which he had been pumping during his monologue.

"Ah, Mr. O'Rourke, 'tis the blarney you have for sure," Kate teased him. "Let me introduce you to Lady Stockton and the rest of the party." When these introductions had been performed, and a great deal of easy flattery had poured forth, accepted in the spirit in which it was given, Kate found that Susan had not forgotten her plans for Mr. O'Rourke. She and Laura changed places inconspicuously while Kate and Mr. O'Rourke discussed various members of his large family. When he turned to include Susan in the conversation, a puzzled frown momentarily creased his brow, but he said politely, "And is this to be your first season?"

Laura, with black hair and green eyes, bearing no resemblance to the honey-blond, blue-eyed Susan, replied demurely, "Yes, sir, and I greatly look forward to it. Just being in London is a treat, after the country, you know." Laura made her home in London and had not the slightest knowledge of country life other than visits to homes of friends there.

Mr. O'Rourke turned to Kate to inquire after her aunt, and Susan and Laura again switched places. The next time Mr. O'Rourke turned to that side he took one look at Susan, seated with her head modestly bowed, and returned his amused gaze to Kate. " 'Tis a pity you have disclosed my sole accomplishment to these young women, darlin'. I do so enjoy exhibiting it. Which of the dears has the honor of being your sister?"

Kate glanced past him to be sure no further change had occurred and informed him that Susan was now seated beside him. He turned to her with a laugh and said, "You are a naughty puss, and I feel sure we shall deal well together. I suppose this is your first season, too. 'Tis a pity the season knocks all the liveliness out of such young dears," he droned sadly, his eyes dancing.

"Oh, Laura, he has caught us already," Susan declared with affected disappointment, and she beckoned her friend to join them.

"And so often we have been told we are as like as two peas in a pod," Laura laughed.

"No more than the truth," Mr. O'Rourke declared stoutly. "When the angels descend they radiate such a glow as one can only perceive their beauty and not the nature of it."

"We are forewarned of your flattery, sir," Laura retorted with a saucy wave of her fan and a mock flutter of eyelashes.

"I have you, no doubt, to thank for this deflation of my pretentions," he grumbled to Kate. "You introduce me to two of the most beautiful women in London only to dash my hopes from the outset."

"I have yet to see you despondent, Mr. O'Rourke," Kate replied musingly. "It must be a most enlightening spectacle."

"Ah, but then you did not see me when last we parted," he rejoined quickly. "Me heart, once a burning sun, turned cold as the winter's ice."

"I am pleased to see that it has recovered its warmth," Kate informed him.

The intermission was ending, and Mr. O'Rourke rose to take his leave, but not before he said, " 'Tis only that you are by again, Miss Montgomery. May I call on you?"

"With pleasure, Mr. O'Rourke."

When he had vanished after his own particular habit, Susan turned to her sister. "I like him. Is he always so full of flummery?"

"Yes, always. But he is so impudent about it that one cannot take it amiss and, frankly," Kate admitted, "I find it very uplifting at times."

15

The next day brought a stream of visitors at tea time. Lord Norris made his restrained every-other-day call; Lady Stockton and Laura were there; all of the Montgomerys were home; and Patrick O'Rourke put in an appearance. Everyone was chatting and, thanks to Mr. O'Rourke, there was considerable laughter, when Sampson appeared at his most dignified to announce the Earl of Winterton. Mrs. Montgomery dropped the biscuit she had just lifted, and Kate turned toward the door with a slight flush. She experienced an inexplicable pride when she saw him, resplendent in a brown broadcloth coat and kerseymere pantaloons, his Hessians and cravat so elegant that she scarcely recognized him. His eyes quickly searched the group and came to rest on her, and though his expression was no less arrogant than usual, there was an intensity in his gaze which caused her to feel decidedly flustered. The room suddenly seemed crowded to her, and yet he was the only person in it of whom she was aware.

As Mrs. Montgomery did not seem capable in her surprise of going forward to greet their guest, Kate assumed the responsibility, hesitantly offering him her cold hand. When he took it, he looked startled to find it so chilled in the warm room.

"Lord Winterton, how nice to see you. I had not

thought you would be in town so soon. Are you completely recovered?''

"Yes, Thomas informs me that it was a mild case.''

"I am sure it did not seem so at the time," she returned sympathetically, though it was necessary for her to bite her lip when she remembered his miserable, spotted face and prickly temper. "Come, let me introduce you to our friends.''

"I cannot stay. I came only to assure myself that you had no trouble finding a printer for the book.''

"Surely everyone here would like to meet you. Is your business so pressing?'' she asked gently.

"No, of course not, but I do not wish to break up your party, Miss Montgomery. Your mother looked quite horrified when I was announced.''

"It was merely the surprise. We had not thought to see you in London.''

"Now I understand. If it had occured to you, you could have instructed your butler to refuse me," he quizzed her.

"Why, I do believe you have a sense of humor, Lord Winterton.'' Kate relaxed somewhat and led him first to her parents and Lady Stockton, with whom he was acquainted through his mother. They progressed to Ralph, Susan, and Lord Norris, who was as incredulous as Mrs. Montgomery at finding his guardian at the Montgomerys'. In fact, it crossed his mind that Winterton had come specifically to seek him out for some reason, and he hurriedly scanned his mind for some misdemeanor.

His alarm was so clearly writ on his countenance that Kate took pity on him. "Lord Winterton has come to inquire after a matter of printing and can stay but a moment. You will excuse us, I hope, if I take him to meet the others.'' Charles was delighted to do so, and

Susan, who went in awe of Winterton, agreed with alacrity. Ralph, however, followed them to where Laura and O'Rourke were talking.

Winterton towered over O'Rourke, but this did not intimidate the elegant Irishman in the least. Laura studied Winterton's rugged features and closed expression and compared them, unfavorably, with O'Rourke's charming, good-natured countenance. She knew that Winterton was a neighbor of the Montgomerys in the country, but it surprised her that he should visit them in town.

Mr. O'Rourke, all unknowing, proceeded to open a very dangerous subject. "I believe I met your brother Carl in London some years ago. A great fellow! How is he?"

Winterton's expression became rather more grim than it had been, and Laura unconsciously shrank back from the group. "He died three years ago of a wound sustained in the Peninsula."

Abashed at this revelation and the tension he felt in the group, Mr. O'Rourke exclaimed, "I am so sorry to hear it! My condolences. I didn't know he had joined up. He made no mention of the possibility."

"He joined the 5th Dragoon Guards in eleven," Ralph offered helpfully, and attempted to keep his eyes from wandering to Kate, who maintained a stiff silence during the exchange.

Winterton, however, could not refrain from glancing at her, and she, impelled by his unspoken reproof, returned his look steadily and said softly, "We all miss Carl. He was a great friend of Ralph's, you know."

"We lost too many good men in the war," Mr. O'Rourke declared. "And now the rest of the poor devils are home, they are more likely to starve than not."

"Very true," Winterton agreed. His grim look relaxed enough to show some interest in what the Irishman was saying. "Can you see any help forthcoming for them from the government?"

"Not a shred," O'Rourke replied despondently. "The government is likely to ignore them altogether."

Ralph fidgeted with his newly acquired quizzing glass, of which he was justly proud, and awaited an opportunity to engage Winterton's attention. It was not in Ralph's nature to be interested in those abstract masses he did not know; he reserved his ready, and very real, concern for those with whom he was acquainted, however scantily. "I say, sir," he finally interrupted. "Have you been to Tattersall's since you came to town?" When the Earl patiently admitted that he had not, Ralph continued enthusiastically, "If you should go there, I hope you will have a look at Lord Cartwright's chestnut. I've a mind to buy him for the farm, and I'd welcome your opinion."

"I daresay I shall look in there in the next few days. I can tell you what I think when next we meet, or send a line round." Winterton turned to indicate to Kate his intention of leaving and found her in animated, joking conversation with O'Rourke. They appeared to be on the friendliest of terms and spoke as old acquaintances. Although Winterton was grievously irritated by O'Rourke's casual familiarity with the young lady, he determinedly remained polite when the Irishman, ever sensitive to a departure, appeared instantaneously beside him to shake his hand and say, "So glad to meet you, Lord Winterton. I hope I shall have the pleasure again soon."

Winterton replied in kind, if with markedly less enthusiasm than his new acquaintance. As Kate walked with him to the bell pull he searched her face for any sign of annoyance with him for his coolness to O'Rourke or his shortness in discussing Carl's death. All he could identify was an unshaken warmth in the brown eyes lifted to his, and he spoke rather gruffly. "You have not as yet told me if I can assist with the printing of the book."

"It is all taken care of; there was no problem at all."

"I'm glad to hear it. Thomas is preparing for your next project—a chandler's shop, I believe. Have you a mind to continue?"

"Certainly. No doubt I shall learn all about tallow or wax or forms and such. I'll make a point of visiting a chandler's while I am here," Kate assured him earnestly, her eyes amused.

"Do you return to the Hall soon?"

"In a few days. Papa has not decided precisely when yet."

"No doubt you will attend Lady Stockton's ball for her daughter."

"Yes, Mama is adamant that I shall. Lady Stockton is a long-time family friend."

"Then I shall look forward to seeing you Thursday."

"*You* are going to Lady Stockton's?" Kate could not conceal her surprise.

"It was my intention," he replied stiffly.

Kate smiled gratefully. "I *am* glad. It will be most . . . *comfortable* to see a familiar face in the squeeze."

"Until Thursday, then." Winterton touched her cheek gently and abruptly took his leave without waiting for Sampson to be summoned.

Bemused, Kate watched the door close behind him, leaving the room once again to its normal proportions, no longer crowded, but empty. Ridiculous to put such significance on his call, on the tiny gesture of . . . friendship? No, he would never choose anyone to be his friend whom he considered less than honorable, as he did her. But there was no need for him to have called at all. If he were interested in the printing of the book, surely he could have had Mr. Single send a note round to inquire. It would have been more in keeping with his dignity. But he had come to see her. Why? She was interrupted in her meditations by an apologetic Mr. O'Rourke.

"So sorry to have spoken of Carl, Miss Montgomery. I had not heard of his death, and Ralph says there is some . . . ah . . . awkwardness about it between you and his lordship. Must be that devilish leprechaun acting up again," he said ruefully.

"There is nothing to be concerned about, Mr. O'Rourke," Kate assured him. "Lord Winterton does not approve of me, but it has not prevented him from being of service to the whole of my family."

O'Rourke regarded her thoughtfully. "I think you are mistaken, Miss Montgomery. Lord Winterton did not appear disapproving, or even indifferent to you. He's not married?"

A flush stained her cheeks, and she made a gesture of denial to his implication. "No. He lives alone at Winter Manor. His mother died about a year after Carl. Lord Norris," Kate said, indicating that young man across the room, "is Lord Winterton's ward."

"Methinks Lord Norris has an interest in your sister," O'Rourke replied laughingly.

"I think you are right. Come, let's save Laura from Ralph's talk of horses."

Lady Stockton's ball, early in the season as it was, could be described only as a crush, which of course was the highest praise one could receive. Laura looked radiantly beautiful in a white satin gown embellished with emerald green ribbons to emphasize her eyes. She knew quite a few of the guests and, feeling relatively at ease in London society, assisted Susan to feel comfortable. Kate attempted to stay in the background; it was Susan's season, and Kate was determined that her sister should enjoy it to the full. Kate, well past the required pale colors and docile behavior of a first season, was able to dress as she pleased in a burgundy silk which became her.

When Mr. O'Rourke claimed Kate for the cotillion, he found her amongst a crowd of gentlemen each intent on describing for her his particular exploits during the previous hunting season. As he led her off on his arm, he proceeded to enlighten her on his own adventures in the hunting field; these prominently included his leprechaun, Sprig. Kate was laughing merrily when she happened to glance to the side of the room, where Lord Winterton had appeared and was regarding her. She flushed slightly, to her annoyance, and nodded to him before the movement of the dance recalled her attention. When the dance was completed and O'Rourke returned her to her mother and Susan, Winterton was there speaking with them.

"Good evening, Miss Montgomery," he said politely, as he bowed. "Your sister has honored me by agreeing to stand up for the boulanger with me. Might I hope that you have the succeeding waltz free?"

"I do and it would be a pleasure, Lord Winterton. Have you been to Tattersall's yet? Ralph is anxious to know what you think of the chestnut?"

"I saw it yesterday, and spoke with your brother a few minutes ago. An excellent animal, and would be a wise addition to his stud."

"Have you been to the farm, then?" Kate asked curiously.

"Several times. Does that surprise you?"

"Yes," she replied frankly, then conceded, "I suppose it should not. You have been most kind to my family."

The music for Winterton's set with Susan was beginning. After a brief, inscrutable look at Kate, he claimed his partner, and Kate found Lord Norris at her elbow to do likewise.

"Makes me nervous finding him around all the time," Charles murmured pathetically.

"Poor Charles. Has he been hard on you?"

"No, and that is what makes me nervous," Charles confessed. "He has been most accommodating to me and even gave me an advance on my allowance. What do you suppose he's up to?"

"I imagine it's just his old age, Charles. Perhaps he's mellowing," Kate suggested, as she picked Winterton and Susan out of the group in the next set. Susan appeared to be listening to him with less than her usual awe. Winterton in fact was putting himself out to be agreeable to her. He had made her known to several of his friends in the set before the dance began and then spoke with her, when they were together, about neighborhood acquaintances, including Lord Norris.

Charles followed Kate's glance and remarked hopefully, "They seem to be going on well, don't they?"

"Much better than usual," Kate agreed. "Susan usually treats him as though he were the Prince Regent and has not a thing to say to him."

"I imagine that's because I've prejudiced her against him," Charles confessed. "But it has been his custom to be rather hard on me!"

"I've no doubt. And he probably would be again if

you were not making such an effort to be the model gentleman. You know, you seem to have matured considerably in the last few months, Charles.''

''Do you think so?'' Charles blushed under her praise. ''Winterton has given over a great part of my estate management to me and, you know, I find I enjoy it.''

''I imagine it is very satisfying work,'' Kate mused wistfully.

The dance ended, and she returned with Charles to her mother, who was relishing the renewal of ancient acquaintances, and, satisfied that her daughters were enjoying themselves and did not lack for partners, saw no necessity to do more than acknowledge their coming and going with a brief, cheerful nod of her head, which sent the dyed ostrich plumes swaying. Winterton and Susan arrived directly, and Charles shepherded Susan off for a taste of the delicacies Lady Stockton had caused to be liberally spread out in another room.

Winterton secured a glass of champagne for Kate with an imperious nod of his head to the tall, elegantly liveried footman who glanced in their direction. ''You do drink champagne, do you not, Miss Montgomery?''

''Whenever I have the chance,'' Kate confided with a smile as she took the glass he offered. She sipped it gratefully, for the room was hot and stuffy from the hundreds of candles burning in the sparkling chandeliers.

''Have you known Mr. O'Rourke long?'' he asked abruptly.

''Aunt Eleanor and I met him in Ireland several years ago. I have seen him a few times in London since then. He's with the Foreign Office now.''

"Would that he were with the Home Office."

Kate considered for a moment as she sipped at the champagne. "Yes," she said thoughtfully. "I see what you mean. But I am sure Mr. O'Rourke is a credit to the Foreign Office, as well as a charming addition to it. And it seems to me that the men in government are seldom placed where their wisdom is most needed."

Piqued by her praise of the Irishman, a note of sarcasm crept into his voice. "You have given the matter a great deal of thought, I suppose."

"So far as my poor, simple female brain will allow, your lordship," Kate retorted. Her hand clenched around the stem of her glass. "I had thought you allowed me a modicum of intelligence, but I see that I was mistaken."

"You were not mistaken, Miss Montgomery. Come, this is our waltz."

Kate was annoyed, but reluctant to deny him the dance she had promised. Could he never deal with her for ten minutes without the arrogance emerging? She wanted to kick him in the shin, but instead allowed him to take her in his arms. She was disturbed by the sensation she felt at his touch. A shyness enveloped her, and she wondered frantically if she could think of anything to say to him. She refused to look at him but pointedly surveyed the whirling mass of elegance about her.

"Are you angry with me?" he asked after a while.

"Yes. No. It cannot matter," she murmured.

Winterton contemplated her averted face, the brown tresses swaying with the movement of the dance. Although her steps did not falter, he could feel the tautness in her body, as though she were straining away from him. He released his hold on her to the merest touch, and her startled eyes met his. "Are you afraid of me?"

"Of course not!" she declared with a defiant sniff, her eyes locked with his.

"Good. If you are not afraid of me and you are not angry with me, why are you not talking with me?"

"I was not aware," she said formally, "that the burden of conversation fell upon me."

"Well, you know, I have few social graces, and if you wish us not to appear singular, I fear you will have to assume the task."

"Very well. What do you think of the coming marriage of Princess Charlotte to Prince Leopold?"

"I couldn't care less."

"Do you think there will be a good harvest this year?"

"No."

"Have you an opinion on the Corn Laws?"

"Yes."

"Well, what is it?"

"They are detestable."

"Why?"

"They will cause further starvation in the countryside."

"Do you think this waltz will ever end?" Kate asked desperately.

"Yes," he laughed. "Has it seemed interminable?"

"You know it has. Why are you doing this to me?"

"Ah, you feel it is my turn to bear the burden. So be it. Do you find your house here comfortable?"

"Yes."

"And is your sister enjoying her season?"

"So far."

"How is Ralph progressing with the farm?"

"Very well."

"Will you drive with me tomorrow afternoon in the park?"

Kate barely managed to suppress a nervous giggle. "You are being ridiculous."

"That does not answer my question, Miss Montgomery."

"If I agree, will you be prepared to converse with me?"

"I shall have Thomas draw up a list of subjects to be discussed."

"Very well, but I shall not go until I see the list," she declared, and raised her eyes to his to add, "I'm glad you're not always stuffy."

"I shall endeavor to be quite light-hearted," he rejoined solemnly. "I may be tempted to stray somewhat from Thomas's list, though, for although an admirable secretary in every way, he is not omniscient and may fail to cover every subject I might be inclined to discuss."

There was a suggestion of intimacy in the words which was not belied by the tenderness in his eyes and the renewed possessiveness of his arm about her. Kate was so shaken by her own response to him that she barely managed to force a lightness to her tone when she said, "I shall be pleased to hear anything you have to say, Lord Winterton. My only fear is that you will have no conversation whatsoever."

"I can think of appropriate moments for that as well," he retorted.

"Well . . . I . . . I cannot," she stammered. "That is, if we are to drive in the park. I mean . . . there might be occasions for silence . . . at the theater, for instance. I should feel most uncomfortable if we were not to speak on a drive."

"No, would you? I give you my word that I will

keep you as comfortable as possible, by whatever means are necessary.'' His amusement at her confusion was kindly, and he pressed her hand encouragingly. "There, you see, the waltz is ending at last.''

"About time,'' she murmured as she placed her hand on his arm to be escorted from the dance floor. Mr. O'Rourke was waiting to take her in to supper, and she did not see Winterton again during the long evening.

16

Although Kate and her family had not returned to the house in Brook Street until the early hours of the morning, Kate rose by mid-morning so famished that she descended to the breakfast parlor to partake of a truly admirable meal. She was alone at this repast when Sampson entered to present her a letter on a silver salver, which she proceeded to open directly, noting that it was from her Aunt Eleanor.

> My dear Kate (it read) I have at last succeeded in discovering Charity's problem. I shall not disclose it to you, as she has merely agreed to explain to Ralph (if he should still be interested, she emphasized) why she felt forced to refuse his offer. If Ralph does decide to come, I hope you will come with him, for Charity could use your support. And I still have not succeeded in ridding myself of Dawson's housekeeper! I want to get this off immediately, so I shall say no more.
>   Your loving aunt, Eleanor

Fortunately Kate had nearly completed her meal, for this epistle sent her dashing off to Ralph's room without delay. When she tapped on the door, there was no response, and she could not discover Walker anywhere about. Her had probably waited up for Ralph and was sleeping as soundly as his master. Kate rapped on the door more vigorously and was rewarded by a grunted, "What do you want?"

"It's Kate, Ralph, and I have some very important news for you. May I come in?"

"Oh, very well," came the merest sigh which Kate established as she entered had been produced from beneath the covers where her brother remained. She flung open the draperies and rang for Walker before seating herself on the edge of the bed. Ralph cautiously lowered the covers to peer out at her, blinking in the bright sunlight. "Nothing," he declared stoutly, "could be important enough to wake me at this hour."

"Read this," Kate urged, pushing the sheet of paper under his nose.

"Can't expect me to read anything in this state," he groaned.

"Read it, Ralph. It's from Aunt Eleanor."

A spark of interest gleamed in his bleary eyes, and he pushed himself up in bed cautiously as Walker arrived at the door. "Some chocolate and toast, please, Walker. And don't blame me for getting you up at this hour. Kate's fault." He reached for the paper Kate extended with his right hand and brushed his tangled blond hair back with the other. He read the letter once, and then again. His eyes, full of tortured hope, sought out Kate's. "Can we leave within the hour, Kate?"

"Yes, Ralph. You will wait until you speak with Charity before setting your hopes too high, will you not, my dear?"

"I'll try. I'm just pleased to be able to see her again," he admitted, swallowing unsteadily.

Leaving Ralph to inform their parents, Kate begged Betsy's assistance in her packing while she sat down to write a note to Winterton. She felt sure that he would not understand her defection. Somehow the drive in the park had assumed large dimensions for her, and she sensed that it was a crucial point in their relationship. With a sigh she dipped the pen in the standish and wrote:

> Dear Lord Winterton, I received a letter from my Aunt Eleanor this morning, and its contents make it imperative that Ralph and I leave for Daventry immediately. I regret that I must break our appointment to drive this afternoon. As I may go straight to the Hall without returning to London, I would appreciate your having Mr. Single obtain the books from Mr. Hicksley, the printer, in Bond Street Wednesday next.
>
> Yours most sincerely, Katherine Montgomery

Kate rang for a footman to deliver the letter straight away to Winterton House and then finished her packing. Her spirits were perhaps lower than they ought to have been. She gave herself a mental shake and went off to bid her parents a hasty farewell.

Winterton was informed that a note had been brought round from Brook Street while he sipped tea in his bed (not quite so elaborate as the one at Winter Manor) and contemplated the afternoon's drive. This intelligence brought an immediate frown, and he lifted the letter from the tray with annoyance. It could be nothing but a cancellation of the drive, and he was loath to read it. He waved his valet out of the room and, holding the letter in a tight grip, contemplated the inscription for some time before breaking the seal. When he had finished reading the short note he crumpled it into a ball and threw it across the room toward the grate. Damn the woman! She must needs leave town to avoid him. To be sure, there was probably a reason to go to Daventry, but the suddenness of it was suspicious. He felt rejected and more than normally cross. He rang for Thomas.

Thomas was sensitive to Winterton's moods, and he knew before his employer spoke a word that he was in a rage. Nor did Thomas miss the crumpled letter near the grate; he retrieved it and made to hand it to Winterton, who shrugged and said, "It contains a message for you. You may read it."

"I shall of course be happy to pick up the books for Miss Montgomery," Thomas commented after he had finished the note. "I believe Miss Martin-Smith resides in Daventry," he mused.

"You think that is why they have gone?" Winterton asked sharply.

Thomas responded blandly, "I have not the slightest idea, sir."

"Oh, go to hell," Winterton rasped, at which Thomas merely smiled. "Why can they not all look after their own affairs without dragging her into them?"

"I believe you have expressed the opinion that she is an interfering wench. That would explain it," Thomas offered.

"Go work on some ledgers!" Winterton growled, tempted to throw his pillow at the grinning secretary.

"Very good, sir."

It was with some difficulty that Kate avoided explaining to her parents why she and Ralph were leaving so abruptly for Daventry. Mrs. Montgomery querulously wondered if her children could not take a day to prepare, as she was sure they would forget half their belongings, and Mr. Montgomery was suspicious as to their errand having something to do with Charity Martin-Smith, but Kate was as calmly evasive as Ralph had been with them. While Ralph paced the entry hall and stretched his driving gloves out of recognition, Kate hugged a tearful Susan and bade her sister see that their mother enjoyed her stay in London. "Don't give her anything to fret over, will you, love? And make my farewells to Mr. O'Rourke and Lady Stockton and Laura." Kate noted Ralph's increased agitation to be off; his hair stood on end once more from his absently running his fingers through it. She put her sister aside with, "Enjoy yourself, Susan. I'll see you at the Hall this summer."

Ralph barely took the time to make his own farewell to his younger sister before he was out the door and seated in the curricle. When Kate was seated he started to thread their way through the London traffic, past brewers' drays and elegant equippages, and they soon left the city noises behind them. At the Green Man he changed teams and made arrangements for his bays to be brought forward to Daventry. When Kate had begun to think that he intended to pass every inn on the road, and allow them to starve, he halted at the red brick White Horse in Hockliffe and ordered a private parlor for them. The landlord brought in coffee, cheese, cold meat, and bread while Kate watched the Holyhead Mail sent off in a flurry of hooves and the arrival of the Chester Mail bound for London.

Ralph took a sip of the coffee, stretched out his legs, and remarked, "We're half-way there now. I suppose it will be too late to see Charity tonight."

"Yes, but you can send a message round to the vicarage that you'll call in the morning."

"Oh, lord, Kate, I've just remembered. I didn't arrange for the purchase of the chestnut before I left."

"Well, Papa will be leaving for the Hall tomorrow or the next day, so it is too late to write him. There will be other horses."

"Yes," Ralph agreed with a grin, "this business is much more important than that."

"Do remember that Charity has only agreed to explain why she rejected you, Ralph. It may be a matter which cannot be overcome," Kate cautioned.

A worried frown creased his brow, but he said nothing then or for the remainder of the journey about Charity. Aunt Eleanor greeted Kate enthusiastically and welcomed Ralph with a concerned warmth that made his sister wonder if he had yet more problems in store for him. Mr. Hall accepted their advent with his usual good humor and applauded their choice of arriving on a day when a beef roast and a raised pigeon pie were available and both still warm in the kitchen.

The Montgomerys soon sat down to a meal, but not before Ralph had scribbled a note to Charity and had it sent round. Aunt Eleanor brought Kate up to date on the happenings in Daventry, and Uncle Hall and Ralph discussed horses.

"I have failed miserably in ridding myself of Dawson's housekeeper. She is an admirable woman and in need of the position, but I really cannot like her," Aunt Eleanor confessed.

"Did you suggest that she take over your old house?"

"I tried, my dear, but she would not hear of such a sacrifice on my part. She has no small conception of her abilities, you understand."

"I daresay. Well, let me think about it a while and see what I can arrange," Kate suggested.

"Anything you can do will be appreciated."

"And I," Kate replied, lowering her voice, "appreciate what you have done for Ralph. I gather there is an obstacle still to overcome, but you cannot know how grateful Ralph is to be given another chance."

Eleanor sighed. "He has a very difficult decision ahead of him, love. I'm glad you came along. How is Susan getting on in town?"

"Very well. Lady Stockton had a ball (was that just last night?) and Susan and Laura were both very well-received. Patrick O'Rourke has been visiting us, too, and the two of them played his own trick on him when first they met. He was decidedly annoyed with me that I had disclosed what he called his one accomplishment." Kate took a sip of her wine and brushed her hair back with a tired hand. "We completed the drive down in good time, but I find that I am wearied with the excitement of the day."

"We'll have you to bed early, then," Eleanor promised. "Was Lord Winterton in town?"

"Yes. We saw him several times."

"Is he pleased with your book?"

Kate's lips twitched at the memory of Lord Winterton's reaction to her book. "He was in his nightshirt when he read it," Kate said mischievously, "and he allowed as how it would do."

"Kate!"

"I'm only teasing you, Aunt Eleanor. He was sick at the time, and Mr. Single chaperoned us quite properly, I assure you. In fact, he seemed delighted with your drawings and said that the book was very good. I left it to be printed in London, and Mr. Single, I hope, will pick it up for me."

"Are you to write more of them?"

"I believe Mr. Single would like me to do one about

a chandler's shop next. I visited one in London, but it was so busy that I could not ask questions. Perhaps Mr. Cofley here will accommodate me.''

''I'm sure he would be happy to do so. He is one of your admirers, you know.''

''And he is a dear.''

''How is Ralph's farm? He deserted it for London?''

''Benjamin was staying on, and Ralph has been pursuing the matter in London. He found a chestnut at Tattersall's that he wanted, but in his hurry to be off here he forgot to arrange to have it purchased for him.''

They adjourned to the parlor and talked for some time before retiring. Eleanor showed them to their rooms and sent a maid to Kate, who expected to sleep the moment her head touched the pillow. Tired as she was, she felt restless. Her thoughts turned to Ralph and Charity, and eventually to Winterton. Really, there was nothing for it but to admit that he was showing an interest in her. Perhaps it meant nothing. For all she knew, it was his standard social practice. But she doubted it. Her defection today would merely fuel his previous disapproval of her, and likely determine him to avoid her in future. She sighed, decided a bit wistfully there was nothing she could do about that, and went to sleep.

Ralph left the house in High Street at ten the next morning, since Aunt Eleanor had informed him that the Martin-Smiths rose early. He was very nervous, and Kate straightened his cravat before he left with a word of encouragement. He smiled solemnly and departed murmuring, ''Wish me luck!''

For all his rush of the previous day he wandered to the vicarage with a notable lack of speed. He was not sure how he should approach this meeting. When he eventually found himself at the door of a vine-covered house with spring flowers poking up all about, he hesitantly knocked and shifted from one foot to the other, still undecided. He was shown into a neat, cheerfully furnished parlor where he found Charity seated, an open book in her lap. Ralph found himself unable to say a word.

Charity rose and smiled a warm greeting at him. "It is good to see you, Ralph. Come and sit by me. I thought you would rather not have to meet my parents and my sister before we talk."

Ralph seated himself stiffly on the chair beside hers and, encouraged by her obvious pleasure in seeing him, said, "Thought I'd never see you again, Charity. I have no right to expect explanations, I know, but I'm very grateful you'd see me. Kate and I drove up immediately we had Aunt Eleanor's letter."

Charity took a deep breath and looked down at her hands which lay quietly in her lap. "Ralph, your Aunt Eleanor has been most kind to me, and it was she who convinced me that you have the right to judge for yourself if I did right to refuse you."

Ralph shrugged helplessly. "I want to marry you, Charity. I'm very fond of you, but I can see I'm no bargain. I don't blame you if you don't want to marry me."

Charity's face flushed softly. She, too, made a helpless gesture with the hands she continued to contemplate and whispered, "And I am fond of you, Ralph. It is not for lack of regard that I refused you. What I am going to tell you now will explain that. Please do not say anything until I am finished. Will you promise me that?"

"Yes," he answered simply, meeting her eyes.

"Years ago I was warned by our family doctor that it is very unlikely that I can have children," she said gently. His shocked expression made her return her gaze to her hands once again. "I made him promise me that he would not tell my family, for I know that it would be very distressing to them." She swallowed unhappily. "I know that you are fond of children and that as the only son you must look to carry on the Montgomery name and estates through your own children. Of course, you might marry someone who did not have children, and you would have to accept that. But I am aware of this problem and therefore could not marry anyone without disclosing it."

"But why did you not tell me?" Ralph asked, his voice agonized.

"Some years ago I was offered for by a nice young man of whom I was rather fond. When I told him, he was very distressed, and I did not see him again. It happened a second time, with the same results, and I decided that it was my own problem and I should not place the burden on any man again. It is a burden I felt I must bear alone." Charity paused for a moment and raised her eyes to his face. "I was unable to bear it alone," she admitted sadly, "and eventually told your aunt. She said you had a right to know. I could not be sure if that was true. I did not wish to hurt you further." A lone tear clung precariously to her eyelash and splashed onto her cheek when she hastily blinked her eyes to clear them.

Ralph jumped from his chair, clumsily drawing his handkerchief from his pocket. He knelt before her and dabbed at the tear-stain. "You silly goose!" he exclaimed. "Of course a family is important, but it is not as important as having you."

Charity stared at him in amazement. "You cannot know what you are saying! Your parents, even your sisters, would be very distressed. You have not thought, my dear.''

"Listen to me, my love. As you say, I could marry someone who did not have children, without ever knowing beforehand. But I do not want to marry anyone but you. There are sufficient Montgomerys in England already. Who cares what happens to my property when I am dead? Surely I cannot. Charity, we have years and years ahead of us. Kate and Susan can bring their children to us for visits; I'm sure they'll have tons of 'em. We might even come in the way of adopting a child.''

"Oh, Ralph, you must want a son of your own to teach to ride, to hunt, to carry on the name and the estates. You are not considering!''

"I know only that if you'll marry me I shall be the happiest of fellows," Ralph proclaimed steadily. He smiled at her and took her trembling hand in his two firm ones. "Please say you will.''

"You must discuss it with your parents. They would not approve," she faltered.

"This is a matter for me alone to decide," he said firmly. "And I have made my decision.''

Charity smiled tremulously at him and touched his cheek gently with a shaking finger. "For my sake, I would have you think on it for a day. I shall not be angry if you change your mind. It were better that you did now than after we are wed.''

"Then you will marry me?" he cried exultantly.

"If you are of the same mind tomorrow, yes, my dear, I will marry you. But I beg that you will give it serious thought. It is a very important decision and one not to be taken lightly.''

"All right," she said solemnly. "I shall consider

the matter thoroughly and return tomorrow at the same
time to see you.''

"You might discuss it with Kate. She will see the
wisdom of what I have told you, and may be able to
convince you of your folly.'' She smiled shyly at him
and rose. "And do not be distressed to come to me
tomorrow with a different decision. I shall perfectly
understand.''

"You are the most wonderful of women, Charity. I
shall see you tomorrow.'' He strode purposefully out
of the room, retrieved his hat, gloves, and cane in the
hall and left the house. Charity stood by the window
and watched him walk down the street, a tender smile
curving her mouth. Even should he change his mind,
she would treasure forever his words of this day. When
he rounded the corner she turned back into the room
with a sigh.

17

Winterton roamed about his townhouse for several hours after the arrival of Kate's note. He should like to have taken his annoyance out upon the servants and Thomas, but he could hear as clearly as though she stood in front of him Miss Montgomery's pert remarks on his disruption of his household when he was sick. He ordered that his favorite stallion be brought round and took himself off for a ride in the park. The spring day showed signs of impending rain now, but the grass smelled fresh and there were flowers blossoming here and there along the way. It was possible for moments at a time to imagine oneself back in the country when one heard the trill of the birdsong.

After a half-hour's ride Winterton came upon his ward and Miss Susan, her friend Laura, and Mr. O'Rourke. They hailed him and he reined in to ride with them for a moment. "I understand your sister and brother have gone to Daventry, Miss Susan," he remarked.

"Why, yes," Susan replied, surprised. "They left but a few hours ago."

"I hope there is nothing amiss."

"Really, they were very mysterious," Susan volunteered ingenuously. "But I am sure nothing is wrong with Aunt Eleanor or her husband, or I would have been told."

"As you say," Winterton agreed. "Did Ralph arrange to purchase the chestnut?"

Susan looked puzzled. "I have no idea, Lord Winterton."

"Ask your father, if you will. If he leaves before sale day, I can see to the matter."

"That is kind of you, sir. I will speak with him."

Winterton turned his attention to his ward for a few agreeable words, and then dropped back to ride beside Laura and O'Rourke. "A very successful ball, Miss Laura. My compliments to your mother."

"Thank you, Lord Winterton. I must admit that I enjoyed it myself." She smiled shyly at O'Rourke, who grinned in return.

"Sure an' the *ton* keep extravagant hours," O'Rourke teased her. "The poor working fellow has not time for any sleep at all."

"But there is always time for a ride," Winterton remarked, with a smile to take the edge off his words.

"If there were not," O'Rourke remarked resolutely, "I would not work."

Laura giggled, and Winterton acknowledged the justice of such a philosophy. He then bade the young people farewell and rode out, leaving them to discuss him.

"He did not used to be so friendly," Susan confided to Charles.

"Don't I know it! Kate says he must be mellowing in his old age, but whatever it is, I cannot object. You don't know why Kate and Ralph went to your aunt's?"

Behind them the other couple, who had only recently met Winterton, were likewise commenting on his lordship.

"Not so easy-going as his brother Carl was, of course," O'Rourke commented sadly, "but not such a bad fellow, either. He seems to have adopted the Montgomerys."

"They are neighbors, and Susan told me that Ralph and Carl were the greatest of friends," Laura remarked.

"I suppose that might be it," O'Rourke said dubiously, and they rode on discussing other matters.

That evening Winterton was brought round a note from Brook Street, sent by Mr. Montgomery this time, in response to Susan's query. He informed Winterton that he was returning to Montgomery Hall in the morning. Ralph had been in a hurry when leaving and had not mentioned the chestnut, so Mr. Montgomery did not know for sure whether he had intended to purchase the animal. He thanked Lord Winterton for his offer of assistance, but allowed as how he thought he would let the matter ride.

Winterton *did* know that Ralph intended to purchase the animal, for he had said as much the previous evening. But Winterton assured himself that he was not responsible for that young man's carelessness. And Miss Montgomery would see, if the matter ever came up, that he had done his best for Ralph by his offer of assistance. Drat the chit! What the hell did he care what she thought about him? One more note was crumpled, and this time it successfully landed on the burning grate.

When Ralph returned to his aunt's home he inquired for Kate straightaway and was informed that she was in the garden. He found her there with a basket over her arm snipping some spring flowers for the house. She turned at his footsteps and anxiously surveyed his countenance. There was an air of suppressed excitement about him, thinly veiled by a mock serious expression.

"Come and sit with me, Kate. Promised Charity I'd give you a chance to dissuade me," he said with a grin.

"Dissuade you from marrying her? Why?"

"She can't have children," he provided succinctly.

Kate regarded him with fascination. "And that does not bother you?"

"Of course it bothers me. Not enough not to marry her, though. Lord, Kate, Aunt Eleanor never had a solitary chick. Lots of women never have any. Only difference is that Charity knows. She's been offered for twice, and both of them were scared off by it. I love her, Kate."

Kate sighed. "I know you do. She has agreed to marry you, then?"

"If I don't change my mind by tomorrow, she will. Told her I'd let you try to talk me out of it. Do your best," he offered handsomely.

Kate laughed. "Silly fellow. Mama and Papa will be disappointed about the children, of course, but they are very fond of Charity. What else did she say?"

"She was concerned that I like youngsters, but I told her you and Susan would share yours with us."

"How thoughtful of you," Kate murmured.

"And of course she worried about the name and the estates. Well, it's not as though there was a title to pass on, you know, and I don't believe it would matter to me if there were. I told her there were sufficient Montgomerys in the country."

Kate leaned over to hug her brother and plant a salute on his cheek. "Oh, Ralph, I am so proud of you."

Ralph's embarrassment was obvious, but he managed to mutter, "Thank you, my dear. Will you come with me to choose a ring for her? I don't know the least thing about such baubles. Like to take it with me tomorrow."

"Of course. We can go right now." Kate hesitated for a moment. "You do not want to discuss it with Aunt Eleanor or Uncle Hall?"

"No, dear girl. I only promised to speak with you for Charity's sake. Told her it was my decision. And it is, you know."

"Yes, Ralph, and a very good one," Kate said as she rose with a smile. "Let's be off."

The next morning Charity was seated once more in the parlor alone. She clenched her hands nervously when she heard the knock at the door and forced herself to remain seated until Ralph was ushered into the sunlit room.

He smiled at her and unceremoniously thrust a jeweler's box into her hands, saying only, "Open it, my love."

Her eyes sparkled with tears as she lifted the lid to find a magnificent emerald ring. "Know I should have asked your father's permission first, but in the circumstances . . ." He placed the ring on her finger and clasped her to him. She sobbed against his shoulder, and he dug once more for a handkerchief. "No more tears, love. I'm running out of handkerchiefs."

Charity gave a teary chuckle and smiled shyly. "Oh, Ralph, I am so happy. You are sure?"

"Never more so. Love you, you know."

Charity's lips trembled, but her eyes sparkled joyfully as she sighed, "And I love you. I never did anything so difficult in my life as refuse you at the Hall."

Ralph kissed her shyly and felt near to bursting with his happiness. After a moment he stepped back and said firmly, "I should talk with your father. Is he here?"

"I shall take you to him in the library. I have told him about you, Ralph, but I did not tell him you offered for me at the Hall. Of course he knows your aunt and uncle and Kate. You need not mention the . . . problem. I will speak with my parents about that later." They were at the library door, and Ralph made an ineffective effort to straighten his cravat. Charity worked it into place and tapped on the door. They were bidden to enter.

Ralph was relieved at sight of the gentle cleric who rose to greet them. "This is my papa, Ralph. Papa, Ralph Montgomery, Kate's brother."

"How do you do, sir? I hope we don't intrude?" Ralph asked conscientiously.

"Not at all," Mr. Martin-Smith said with a smile. "I have heard of you from your sister and aunt, and of course from my daughter." Seeing that Ralph was feeling rather awkward, he asked kindly, "Is there something I can do for you?"

"With your permission, I should like to marry Charity," Ralph blurted.

"Well, that is straightforward enough," Mr. Martin-Smith admitted with a smile.

Charity said gently, "I have accepted him, Papa. We want your blessing and Mama's. I will leave you now to talk with Ralph." She gave Ralph a reassuring squeeze of the hand and a smile before she departed.

"I beg your pardon, sir. Didn't mean to be so . . . abrupt. I have the highest regard for your daughter," Ralph stammered.

"Sit down, young man. If I recall the procedure correctly, I should now ask you of your prospects. Is that right?"

Ralph grinned. "Daresay it is. Never been through this before, you understand." And he proceeded to enlighten Charity's encouraging father about himself, his family, and his "prospects." Mr. Martin-Smith then sent for his wife and introduced Ralph to her.

"I have approved Mr. Montgomery's offer for Charity," he informed her, "and have given them my blessing. Charity," he said, with dancing eyes, "has already accepted him."

"I am so pleased to meet you, Mr. Montgomery. Charity spoke highly of you when she returned to Bath. And Kate is a favorite with all of us, of course." She seated herself and spoke with him for a while, in her soft, calm voice. Ralph was reminded of his beloved. He felt immediately at ease with her, and she was pleased with him.

Charity was sent for, and her father and mother assured her that she had their blessing. "Now be off with you and inform Kate and Mr. and Mrs. Hall," the vicar urged. "And don't forget to discuss when you wish to be married."

It was only a matter of minutes before Kate was hugging her friend and congratulating the radiant couple. Aunt Eleanor and Uncle Hall added their wishes for happiness and suggested that the young couple might like to have some time to themselves in the garden, an offer they gratefully accepted.

When Uncle Hall left them together, Kate and her aunt discussed the outcome. "I was not sure," Aunt Eleanor sighed, "that they would come to this conclusion. Not many young men of family are willing to face the prospect of having no heir."

"I know," Kate replied. "I was very proud of Ralph for his decision. He is very fond of children, and promised Charity that Susan and I would share ours with them.''

''I suppose I am overly sensitive to the subject,'' Aunt Eleanor mused. ''I had expected to present Sir John with innumerable offspring, and I felt for a while that I had failed. But, you know, it did not spoil our lives together. He never reproached me; in fact, there were times when he confessed that he was pleased there were just the two of us.''

''I'm sure he was. You have been very lucky, my dear. Do you suppose Ralph will remember to write our parents?''

''I doubt it. You will have to remind him. I hope you will both stay on for some time so that he and Charity can enjoy getting to know each other better.''

''And so that I can try to rid you of Uncle Hall's housekeeper?''

''That, too, of course,'' Aunt Eleanor admitted with a grin.

''I think I had best start on the project, now that I am not needed to provide support to either Ralph or Charity. Tell me about the tenant you have found for your old house.''

Kate was frequently invited to join Charity and Ralph on their expeditions, and occasionally she accepted. At other times she visited the various shops, especially the chandler's, and delved into their workings, making notes and urging her aunt to do some drawings for her. She assisted Mr. Martin-Smith with the parish work Charity usually did in an effort to free her friend's time. And she set about her most important task, freeing her aunt from Uncle Hall's dreaded housekeeper.

Since Mrs. Higgins was a model housekeeper and

was not willing to take Eleanor Hall's hints that she exchange places with Mrs. Moore, Kate determined on a strategy where Mrs. Higgins would suggest the change herself. With Mrs. Moore's connivance, the bachelor General's household was allowed to degenerate to the point where he came to Mr. Hall with complaints of the food, lack of heat, and general disorderliness. On hearing of this state of affairs Mrs. Higgins found an excuse to visit her rival's establishment and was genuinely horrified, but Eleanor Hall would hear nothing of her dire comments, saying agitatedly, "To be sure, but you must understand that Mrs. Moore is used to instruction. She cannot handle everything without guidance, and I was used to give it to her."

When Eleanor found it necessary to go around to the General's each day and offer Mrs. Moore a guiding hand, it was left to Kate to assume her aunt's responsibilities at home, and she had a few suggestions to make based on her experience at the Hall. Several days of this new regime led Mrs. Higgins to seek an interview with her mistress in which she offered what she thought might prove a solution to the problem, and so the two housekeepers were finally switched.

18

Letters arrived regularly from London, both before and after Ralph's announcement to his family. Mrs. Montgomery proclaimed her joy at the news; Susan wrote that she could not ask for a better sister-in-law. Mr. Montgomery's letter from the Hall was enthusiastic. He alone had been advised of the probability of a childless marriage, and his acceptance of this situation was enough to bring tears to Charity's eyes when Ralph showed her the letter. "You father is such an understanding man," she confided to Kate. "I hope your mother will be able to accept it, too."

"Never fear, my love," Kate assured her. "Mama is so pleased that I doubt anything could diminish her happiness. Ralph will tell her when next he sees her."

Kate had received a letter from her father as well, in which he disclosed his intention of buying Benjamin Karst out of the farm as a wedding present for Ralph. Benjamin, he informed her, was not adverse, as the new endeavor had inspired him with an interest in his Yeovil estate and he had recently determined to see to its management himself for a time. Mr. Montgomery urged Kate to return to the Hall so that she could assist with the farm until Ralph returned.

"So you see, Aunt Eleanor, I must leave once again.

I have enjoyed my stay tremendously, but I long to be in the country for a while.''

"Kate love, you have been of no small service to me.''

"Well, I daresay we all relished our acting abilities for a few days there. I'm glad Mrs. Moore is with you once again. It certainly feels more comfortable with her around. And I am sure the General will do better with Higgins.''

"He has already professed himself quite overcome by her efficiency,'' Aunt Eleanor sighed. "And when I walked over the other day to see how she was going on, she actually preened at her establishment. Frankly, for all her stubbornness, I think she'll be far happier there.''

"No doubt.'' Kate wandered about the room, touching the Staffordshire figures and the Sheraton cabinet brought from her aunt's home. She could not help remembering the years they had spent together, travelling at times and then returning to enjoy life in Daventry. She knew her aunt was happy now, and she was pleased for her. But Kate herself was feeling restless and displaced, and she wished to return to the Hall. "If you can lend me a maid, Aunt Eleanor, I think I will leave tomorrow.''

"So soon, my dear?'' Her aunt eyed her with concern. "You would not rather wait until Ralph is ready to leave?''

Kate smiled suddenly. "Heaven knows when that may be! If he follows his inclination, he will remain here until they wed in August.''

"I feel sure your father will bid him home for some time before that.''

"Of course. And he will have things to see to there.

But I would be off now, and I do not wish to rush him.''

"As you will, dear. Trudy would welcome the trip, I am sure.''

Kate left, as she intended, the following day in spite of protests from Ralph and Charity. She hugged her friend warmly and told her she had spent much longer than she intended already, for May was fast advancing.

"It will not be long now before I have you as a sister and see you frequently,'' Kate said. "And I shall return early for the wedding to be of whatever help I can to you. Papa could use some company now.''

"Yes, I am being selfish,'' Charity admitted. "Have a safe trip, my dear.''

When the maid Trudy had fallen asleep in the post-chaise across from her, Kate retrieved from her reticule the letters she had received from Susan. Her sister's accounts of the London season were filled with balls, routs, cards parties, picnics, and rides in the park with Lord Norris. Patrick O'Rourke and Laura were much in each other's company, which alarmed Lady Stockton a bit, Susan thought. Mama was thriving on the attention she was receiving from her old friends, and Susan made sure that she did not exhaust herself. They saw Lord Winterton frequently, and he was ever pleasant to them, Susan commented wonderingly. Kate returned the letters to her reticule and gazed out the window.

"What the hell are we doing in London, Thomas?'' Winterton asked his secretary one day.

"I think we are looking out for Miss Susan, sir,'' Thomas replied blandly.

"The devil you say! My ward is doing an admirable job of that, without the least need of any assistance. I expect him to appear any day to ask my permission to wed the girl.'' Winterton paced about the room slapping his gloves against his buff-colored pantaloons. ''I'm fatigued with all the simpering beauties and gambling dandies. Did you send Miss Montgomery's book off to the school?'' he asked abruptly.

''Several weeks ago. We have received a grateful letter from Mr. Collins. I put it with your other letters,'' Thomas replied with mock reproach.

''We shall return to the Manor tomorrow,'' Winterton ordered.

''As you wish, sir. Should I send the usual regrets to the hostesses you will be depriving?''

''Certainly.'' Winterton turned to leave, but Thomas stayed him.

''I don't believe you've seen the *Morning Post* as yet.''

''No.''

''There is an announcement which might interest you,'' Thomas replied and folded the paper to the required reading before he handed it to his employer.

For a fraction of a second Winterton felt a painful anxiety which was instantly relieved when he perceived that the Montgomery name in the announcement was Ralph's. ''She brought it off,'' he snorted and calmly returned the paper to his secretary. ''We will make an early start in the morning. And, Thomas, send round a note to the Montgomerys asking if we can convey any messages from them to the Hall.''

Kate's journey was uneventful, and she arrived in good spirits at the Hall. Mr. Montgomery greeted her with his usual warmth and immediately involved her in his transactions for Ralph's farm. They spent a lengthy time discussing Ralph's engagement and the plans which were being made for the wedding. Kate asked for the latest news from the rest of the family in London.

"Your mama and Susan write nothing but raves of their entertainments there. They will be home in June, after town thins for Brighton. I think your mother misses me, for all the fun she's having. Perhaps I will join them for the last week or two and see them home. Would you like to do that?"

"Perhaps. I must think about it and let you know when the time gets closer, if you don't mind."

"Certainly. I imagine you would rather not contemplate another trip when you have just arrived home," Mr. Montgomery suggested.

Kate spent several days pursuing those delights she could not taste so well in Daventry—gallops across the meadows, driving a team into the village, gardening in her mother's sadly neglected flower patches. Benjamin Karst rode over to inform them that he had signed the necessary papers and was off to Yeovil "to make my fame and fortune," as he told Kate when they strolled through the gardens, seeking shade. The sun was beating down unmercifully for so early in the season, and Benjamin did not allow his horse to stand for long. He placed an awkward salute on her cheek, promised to write, and begged her to offer Ralph his most sincere congratulations, before he waved his farewell.

Squinting in the sunlight to watch his retreating figure, Kate remembered a slender, ancient volume that she had found when travelling in France, and she immediately ascended to her room to dig it out from her other travel mementoes. This took a little time, as she had never spent the necessary hours organizing her treasures, but she came at last upon the book by

M. Thevenot. Tucking it into her reticule, she went to the library to inform her father that she was riding over to Ralph's farm and would return in time for dinner. He absentmindedly acknowledged her remarks and returned to his work.

Kate rode slowly, for the oppressive heat affected even the sorrel mare. As she progressed she kept half an eye on the lane and half an eye on the book she had started to peruse. The volume was called *L'Art de Nager,* and Kate was fascinated by the idea of learning to swim. She had once seen a man drown for lack of anyone being able to rescue him, and had purchased the book some two years before on an impulse. Aunt Eleanor had teased her that females were allowed only the ridiculous bathing machines at the coastal resorts but Kate had retorted, "One day I shall learn to swim." Her aunt had cautioned her not to drown in the process, and had thought no more of it.

Upon reaching Ralph's farm, Kate rode about for a while and checked the progress of the improvements and the state of the fields. A hard spring and more rain than usual had not been felicitous, but the new drainage was a help. When she was satisfied that all was in reasonable order and that there were no men working anywhere near the stream she seated herself on the bank and practiced the movements suggested by the book. It was exceedingly awkward in her lengthy skirts and, taking one last look about her, she removed the blue muslin riding habit and found the one-piece under garment of muslin with its vest and footed drawers much more comfortable for her chosen activity.

Kate stepped into the icy stream and yelped "Jupiter!" rather dramatically before she became used to the temperature of the water. Actually, she acknowledged to herself, it was quite refreshing after the intolerable sun. She carefully tested the depth of the stream and found that she could stand easily all the way across, though the boulders which were strewn over the bottom did not make easy walking for her tender feet. When Kate had wandered downstream a bit and found the deepest spot she could, she attempted to put into practice what she had been reading. It was not so easy as it sounded. Somehow one was expected to coordinate the thrusting forward together of the arms with a quite ludicrous frog-like kick of the legs, quickly following. And this, she thought bitterly, is supposed to keep me afloat. She swallowed a large mouthful of water and struggled to her feet.

Undaunted, she continued to pursue her attempts until she was managing two or three strokes in a row and was only partially sunk each time. After a while she seated herself on a large sunny boulder and let the sunlight filtering through the trees on the banks warm her. I shall have to work on this for some time if I am to master it, she thought, and the weather is not always so fine. So she determined to work on the stroke a bit longer. As she stepped into the stream once more her foot slipped and she was tossed into the water, her foot lodged between two stones.

Winterton, who had been peacefully dozing over his fishing pole in the hot sun when he heard Kate's exclamation upon entering the water, had been roused to wakefulness and had thoroughly enjoyed her self-taught lesson. He was seated some distance down the stream, his boots negligently kicked off, and he had not intended to make himself known. Her struggles galvanized him, however, and she found strong arms lifting her head and releasing her foot. He scooped her up and placed her on the bank in the sun, brushing the dripping hair out of her eyes. She looked at him, grimaced, and said, "Aunt Eleanor warned me not to drown myself."

He returned her gaze, noting the muslin garment transparent in its wetness, and exclaimed, "For God's sake, Kate, put some clothes on!"

Kate, unaware of how revealing her outfit was, rose unsteadily to her feet and immediately walked away from him, saying haughtily, "Thank you for your assistance, Lord Winterton."

Although Winterton wished nothing more than to assure himself that she was all right and to soften his hasty words, he did not dare follow her in her all-but-nude state. His view of her from a distance had been alluring in the cling of the muslin to her body; but he had not been alarmed until he had seen her out of the stream. He watched helplessly as she walked angrily away from him and, since even this view was altogether unnerving, he turned away and stomped across the stream to regain his boots.

Kate, in high dudgeon, flung on her riding habit, retrieved her horse and book, and rode back to the Hall, heedless of her condition. It was not until she reached her room, careful to avoid everyone in the household, that she relieved herself by swearing in the cheval glass as she changed out of her now-damp riding habit. She was arrested by the sight she presented. An alarming blush crept from her neck to the roots of her hair. Oh, God, she thought as she looked on her revealed body. I can never face him again. She stripped the clinging muslin from her and wrapped herself in a towel, as she rubbed furiously with another at her damp hair. How could I be so skip-brained!

Kate managed to maintain a conversation with her father at dinner on the improvements at Ralph's farm, but she excused herself soon after to retreat to her room. The scene at the stream went through her mind again and again, each time bringing a blush to her cheeks. She attempted to interest herself in a book, only to put it aside again. At last, before the sun went down, she crawled into bed like a wounded animal and was rewarded by the unconsciousness of sleep.

Since it was raining the next morning, her first intent, to take a ride, was doomed to disappointment. She rang for her chocolate and sat long in bed sipping it. He would call today. There was really no doubt about it. She could have him refused. That was what she wanted to do, but the hard core of shame of yesterday had given way to a milder embarrassment, as it will when an event is run over frequently enough in the mind. She sighed and determined that she would see him. Much better to get it over with. Reluctantly she climbed out of bed and donned the most demure frock she owned, a flush on her cheeks.

It was an enormously long morning. She dawdled over breakfast, discussed the days work with the upper housemaid who substituted while Butterfield was in London, played the dulcimer softly, and finally wandered into the parlor with a book. When a footman arrived to announce Lord Winterton, she was *almost* relieved.

He was rather formally dressed in elegant calling clothes, which stirred a memory in Kate. She could not prevent the blush which colored her cheeks, but she met his eyes unwaveringly. Her greeting was polite and her suggestion that he seat himself accepted. She had seen him suave, had seen him cold, had seen him biting and bitter, and even seen him friendly. She had never before seen him awkward, not even when she had found him in a sheet.

"I trust you have suffered no ill?" he asked.

"None."

"I have inadvertently compromised you," he stated abruptly, "and I have come to ask you to marry me."

"Fiddlesticks!" she retorted with heat. "Perhaps *I* compromised *you,* but I dare say it is not the first time you have seen a . . . woman's body." Her color rose alarmingly. "No one knows of the incident, and I feel certain that no one ever will."

"Nonetheless it was a most improper situation for us to be in."

"Do not trouble yourself over the matter, Lord Winterton. It can be forgotten."

"Can it? I doubt it. Come, Miss Montgomery, it is the sensible course for you to marry me. Who knows, perhaps a laborer or farm boy was wandering by. The tale could even now be spreading in the neighborhood."

Kate raised her chin. "I shall have to take that chance. I checked quite carefully before I got into the water that there was no one around."

"You did not see me."

Kate put cold hands to her burning cheeks, and her voice came softly, "You were watching me the whole time?"

"I was fishing. That is, I had fallen asleep over my pole. I heard you exclaim when you got in the water."

"And you did not leave? I find that reprehensible."

"I . . . suppose I should have done so. I assure you I was a considerable distance downstream and . . . could not see more than . . . that you were playing in the water."

"I was not playing," Kate flung at him furiously. "I was teaching myself how to swim."

"Yes, I know. I will teach you to swim."

"I don't want you to teach me! I want you to leave

me alone. I am so mortified! Can't you see?'' she cried
in agony.

He stood and took her hands in his, gently. ''There
is no need to be. As you say, it is not the first time I
have seen a woman so. You were very understanding
to me the day you found me in Small Street. I would
only return the favor.''

Kate smiled crookedly up at him. ''Then let us have
no more talk of marriage, Lord Winterton. It is unnecessary. I shall consider it tit for tat.''

''And if someone witnessed the scene?''

''I doubt even marrying you would prevent *that* gossip. I shall take my chances.''

''I would rather you did not. I am fully prepared to
marry you.''

Kate tried to read his inscrutable face. ''A poor ba-
sis for marriage, my lord. I have other ideas of what
a marriage should be.''

''Such as?''

''For one, mutual respect.''

''I hold you in high regard.'' He witnessed her
flashing eyes. ''Yes, there *is* the matter of the inheritance from Carl. As it would become mine on marriage, I would see that it is usefully disposed of.''

''Never! You shall never touch that money!'' she
threw at him.

''You should not have accepted it, or you should
have disposed of it in a worthy cause,'' he snapped at
her.

''You know nothing of the matter, you . . .'' Kate
could not think of an epithet strong enough to do justice to her emotions.

''It was not honorable to accept it,'' he said flatly.

Winterton was fully unprepared for the ringing slap
she dealt him. When she made to do it again, he caught

her wrist in a grip of steel. "That is enough. You should have thought to defend your honor before you accepted my brother's legacy."

"Release me."

He loosed her hand, but his eyes remained watchful.

Kate glared at him and said, "Wait here. I have something you may be interested in." She spun away from him and hurried from the room. Winterton watched her departure in amusement mixed with despair. He seated himself not altogether comfortably and awaited her return, his eyes wandering to the ormolu clock on the mantelpiece. She was gone exactly four and a half minutes.

Kate thrust two well-worn sheets of paper into his hands and commanded, "Read it, and then leave!"

Winterton regarded her with puzzled eyes. He had immediately recognized his brother's handwriting. Kate said again, "Read it!"

Winterton dropped his eyes to the sheets in his hands and read:

My dearest Kate, I had hoped that I would make it home so that I might see you again and beg your forgiveness. It is not to be; I know I am dying. I have learned many things since I left home, the most important of which is that I treated you dishonorably. There is not another officer I know who could have done such a thing and I am thoroughly ashamed of myself. I was used to having anything I wanted; Mother and Andrew were perhaps too kind to me. I beg you will disregard the foolish, miserable things I said—my death is of course in no way your blame. I have made a will with a bequest to you which I *pray* you will accept as a token of for-

giveness of me. I cannot bear to think of Andrew
and Mother knowing of my villainy, but you are
to tell them if you think best. I can write no
more. God bless you. All my love, Carl.

Winterton sat perfectly still after he finished reading
the letter. He did not raise his eyes when he asked in
a choked voice, "He tried to blackmail you into marrying him? By saying his death would be your fault?"
"Yes."
"And you never told me? Why?"
"Because I knew it would hurt you. You were so
proud of Carl. And you should have been. He made a
mistake, but he is forgiven. I hope you will forgive
him, too."
"I spoiled him. He was young when Father died;
but that is no excuse. I have been much harder on my
wards."
"They will reap the benefits of it."
"Do your parents know?"
"No, but my father has a very fine sense of honor,
too, Lord Winterton, and he wrote me that I should
not accept the money. I was in Daventry then. You had
found the sealed letter after I left, and forwarded it on
to me, with the scathing note you wrote after reading
the will. I assured my father that I had received a last
letter from Carl in which my acceptance of the legacy
was his dying request. I told him that *my* sense of
honor demanded that I accept it, and he made no further objection."
"He would of course accept your word, for he knows
you well and respects you."
"I did, however, tell Aunt Eleanor and Charity,"
Kate continued. "They will allow the information no
further. I was upset when I went to them at Daventry,

you understand. Before Carl's letter arrived I was badly shaken. You must realize that I was not yet twenty and for all my bravado in telling him before he left that it was his own decision to join the fighting and I would not hold myself responsible in the event of his death, I could not but believe that if I had married him he would be alive.''

Winterton's hands were clenched in fists on his knees. The letter dropped unheeded on the floor, and Kate carefully retrieved it and held it tightly. Winterton finally shifted his gaze to her; she had never seen such anguish in a man's eyes before.

''I have no right to ask your forgiveness,'' he said painfully. ''I have wronged you even while you were trying to protect me from this knowledge. I am responsible for Carl's . . . villainy, too. I will not trespass on your kindness longer.'' He rose heavily and bowed to her.

''One moment,'' Kate stayed him. ''I only told you now because I . . . could no longer bear your scorn. That was weak of me, for I had never intended to betray Carl and cause you this agony. You have no need of my forgiveness; I have understood all along, you must realize, why you felt as you did. I have chafed under it, but I did not blame you for that so much. But lately . . . it has hurt me, and I did not think Carl would wish me to suffer for his mistake. It was your haughtiness and bitterness that used to make me angry. But you have been kind to me and to my family, and that is all forgotten. I cannot bear for you to leave without hearing that you forgive your brother.''

Winterton hesitated as he searched her troubled eyes. ''I can do no less if you have forgiven him,'' he said at last.

Kate smiled. ''Thank you, Lord Winterton. You

have made my very happy.'' She extended her hand to him and he grasped it firmly. She suddenly remembered why his attire had stirred a memory in her. His younger ward had dressed just so carefully when he had come to propose to her. To avoid the confusion this caused her, she abruptly changed the subject. "Will you send Mr. Single to me again? Aunt Eleanor and I did some work in Daventry, and I would appreciate his assistance.''

"He has been looking forward to discussing your next project. We did not realize until yesterday that you had returned to the Hall. He can bring your copies of the book; I think you will be pleased with the finished product. Mr. Collins was most appreciative.'' There seemed nothing more for him to say, so he murmured, "I can see myself out.''

19

When Mr. Single came to visit Kate, he brought her the extra copies of her book which she had ordered, including one for her Aunt Eleanor. After discussing the materials Kate had gathered for the next book and reaching a satisfactory direction for the text, Mr. Single took her in the Earl's barouche to visit his brother and family in Stasby. Kate was able to satisfy her curiosity about the reading lessons the vicar's wife gave and to meet her sister, who seemed to be a special object of interest to Mr. Single, Kate noted with a grin. On their drive back to the Hall their discussion turned to Winterton.

Mr. Single had dropped his bantering tone and commented, "He returned from the Hall the other day . . . disturbed. You did not see fit to give him another trimming, perchance?"

"No, nothing like that," Kate answered vaguely.

Thomas knew when he was being warned off the subject, and he had only broached the matter at all in the hope of understanding the reason for the stricken countenance Winterton had presented that afternoon on his return. Winterton, who was often wont to confide in him, had been equally vague. It was not simple curiosity which prompted Thomas; he was sincerely attached to his employer and was disturbed to find him obviously upset. The only information Winterton had imparted was a flat statement that Miss Montgomery had accepted Carl's legacy at his dying request and had done so properly. He had not elaborated on this. In itself it was such a turnabout that Thomas was sure there was more to it, but he had made no effort to press Winterton. "I'm glad you have settled your differences," Thomas now said simply to Kate.

"He told you so? I suppose he felt he must if he had made you privy to his previous beliefs," Kate mused.

They had arrived at the Hall, and Kate said, "I have taken up far too much of your time today, Mr. Single, but I am grateful to you." She started to ascend the stairs, and then bit her lip and turned to him again. "I know you are fond of Lord Winterton and that you will help him just now. If I . . . can do anything . . . I hope you will let me know."

"I shall, Miss Montgomery," he said seriously. When she had entered the house he returned to the barouche, thinking furiously. Good God, had he offered for her and been refused? Somehow his employer's distress had seemed linked with Carl's legacy to this young woman. It was no use trying to figure it out; he would have to content himself with keeping Winterton busy.

Thomas arrived at the Manor to find his employer returning from a ride. "You found Miss Montgomery well?" Winterton asked.

"Very well. We discussed another book, and I took her to visit my brother and talk with his wife about the reading lessons she gives. Miss Montgomery had expressed an interest in teaching her maid to read."

"And how are things at the vicarage? You sister-in-law has not produced the next Single as yet, has she?"

"Not for a month or so. All are well there. Her sister plans to spends the entire summer with them," Thomas said casually.

"I must give you more free time."

They were strolling to the house now, and Thomas regarded his employer suspiciously. "I should not take it amiss," he finally remarked.

"Did Miss Montgomery . . . oh, hell, Thomas, come into the library with me." Winterton handed his gloves and hat to the butler before proceeding through the house to his own private retreat, redolent with the smell of leather. He seated himself, stretched out his long legs, and waved Thomas to another chair. "Did she say anything about the other day?"

"No, she was very reticent, but she voiced her concern for you. I could not help but observe your mood when you returned. I fear I tried to discover its source," Thomas admitted ruefully.

"I would have told you, but it is a matter concerning Carl. He did not treat Miss Montgomery fairly when he was courting her." Winterton attempted awkwardly to circumvent the whole truth.

"He did not seduce her! She was but a child at the time." Thomas was aghast.

"No, no. Nothing of that nature. He . . . attempted to force her to marry him by threatening to join the fighting and get himself killed if she would not." Winterton raked his fingers through his hair. "He begged her forgiveness in a letter he wrote her when he was dying and asked that she accept his legacy as a token of her forgiveness of him. She has suffered much at his hands, and mine," Winterton groaned.

"The young fool!"

"Worse than a fool. It was inexcusable. And yet she has forgiven him, Thomas. What if he had died before writing that letter? That my brother should place such a burden on the girl! That I should have sneered at her for accepting the legacy!''

''You could not know.''

''She could have told me. Anytime these last three years she could have done so. And do you know why she did not? Because she knew it would hurt me.'' Winterton rubbed his brow in an attempt to soothe the headache which would not go away.

''Why did she tell you now?'' Thomas asked curiously.

''Because . . .'' Winterton did not wish to disclose the *whole* of that discussion. ''It stung her that I called her dishonorable.''

''I am shocked that you should do so,'' Thomas said softly.

''She has a way of bringing out the worst in me.''

''And the best.''

Winterton returned the steady gaze. ''As you say. Everything else I know about her is to her credit. This one point had to be . . . clarified. It has been an undercurrent in our . . . in all of our dealings.''

''I'm glad that it has been settled, though I doubt that Miss Montgomery had any joy in doing it.''

''The only joy she received from the interview was in landing me a ferocious slap,'' Winterton said ruefully, as he rubbed his cheek reminiscently. ''No, that is not true. She asked my forgiveness of Carl. I . . . gave it. But it is not something that can be easily forgotten.''

''It must be. You should be grateful that Carl realized his folly before he died. His infatuation with Miss Montgomery unbalanced him somewhat. I did not approve at the time of all the pressure that was brought to bear on her—from you and your mother, as well as

Carl himself. She was scarcely out of the schoolroom. I wonder that she managed to cope with all of it. Her own parents also must have looked kindly on the match.''

"You are not consoling me, Thomas," Winterton said wryly. "I did not wish to play that part, either, but I did not want to see Carl go to the Peninsula in such a frame of mind. He grew up there, though. Cotton spoke most sincerely of his courage and fortitude. And the letter to Miss Montgomery was an agony or realization of his 'villainy.' His wound was not sustained through any rashness, but in the line of duty."

"Be content, then. You owe it to Carl and Miss Montgomery."

"She has every right to hate me."

"You know she does not," Thomas replied firmly.

Winterton did not reply but gazed out the window as he tapped his fingertips on the chair arms. Thomas, correctly assuming that he was dismissed, quietly exited. His employer sat for a lengthy time considering the situation. He had offered for Miss Montgomery and been refused. That refusal, of course, was based partially on the clumsy pretext he had used to make his offer. At the time, too, he had still believed Miss Montgomery—Kate, for God's sake—he had no intention of talking to himself the way he was forced to talk to others—well, he had still believed Kate had been wrong in accepting Carl's legacy. He had not pursued his proposal owing to what followed.

Winterton was curious as to what other items Kate considered essential to marriage. But he was reluctant to press the matter. He did not wish to remind her of her pursuit by his brother. She had suffered enough at the hands of his family. Far better to stifle his own feelings and allow her to go on her way. He felt quite noble, and rather ill, with this resolution.

When several days passed and Thomas realized that his employer had no intention of calling at the Hall again, he felt it necessary to send a note to Miss Montgomery.

20

Kate spent the days after her expedition with Mr. Single in a flurry of activity. She proceeded with work on the "town" book, obtained her father's permission and surveyed the servants remaining at the Hall as to whether any of them were interested in learning to read, and prepared the schoolroom for the two who eagerly accepted her offer. She began to meet with these two experimental pupils an hour a day, every other day. Since they were members of the household, she accomplished this during the mid-morning when they could be freed from their duties for a short period.

In addition to these activities, she often rode over to Ralph's farm to check on the running of the farm and the stable. She regretted that he had had to pass up the chestnut in London. It would indeed have been a wise addition to his stud. She had discussed with her father the possibility that another property be found for the tenant, so that Ralph and Charity could live in the farmhouse. While her father looked into this matter she considered the remodeling of the building which would be necessary. Ralph was to be home within the next few days, and Charity and her parents would follow in mid-June so that they might meet Mr. and Mrs. Montgomery. Since their visit could not be lengthy, owing to Mr. Martin-Smith's being unable to desert his parish for long, Kate was determined that she would have all organized so that Charity and Ralph could make the necessary decisions in the short period of time they would have.

These activities were not sufficient to keep Kate's mind from wandering to her main preoccupation, of course. She refused to give in to thoughts of Winterton and her refusal of his suit. He had not offered her what she wanted, and she came to fear that he would not, as the days passed without word from him. So she also spent many hours organizing her travel memorabilia and playing the pianoforte and dulcimer for her father in the evenings.

When Mr. Single's note arrived she quietly withdrew to her bedroom to read it. "Dear Miss Montgomery: Knowing of your concern for Lord Winterton's distress, I pen this note to advise you that he has confided to me your revelation of Carl's behavior toward yourself. We had a long discussion of the matter, and I think his mind is much more at ease. There appears to be some other problem troubling him which he has not deemed it advisable to confide to me, and which is causing some distress and withdrawal on his part. I persist in believing that it is something which can be worked out. Where I have failed, perhaps you can succeed. Your most obedient servant, Thomas Single."

Kate was pleased with this message. She continued her activities and welcomed her brother home the next day with enthusiasm. Before he had time to reach his room, she and her father had made him aware of the various activities going forth on his behalf. He was caught up in their enthusiasm and suggested that he and Kate ride over to the farm first thing next morning.

"Benjamin didn't mind selling out?" he wondered.

"No," his father replied. "He is eager to try his own hand on the Yeovil property."

"And you think the farmhouse can be remodeled to suit us, Kate?" Ralph asked eagerly.

"I believe so. You will have to decide. Papa and I have thought of some possibilities. The sooner you decide what is to be done, the sooner the work can be started. Some things can go forward now, and when Charity comes you can complete the arrangements. The project will provide some much needed work in the neighborhood, too."

"Yes," her father agreed. "It will serve a dual purpose. I have found another farm for your tenant, and we will generously reimburse him for the change. Things are in a way to being settled, if they meet with your approval."

"Can't thank you enough," Ralph said, as he shook his father's hand heartily and then hugged his sister.

Ralph and Kate started for the farm directly after breakfast the next day. Kate spent the ride telling Ralph of her projects and soliciting information on Charity and Aunt Eleanor and Uncle Hall. When they arrived, the tenant's youngest son burst into a gleeful smile on sight of Ralph and took to his heels. "I say," Ralph laughed. "What did I do to cause that?" But they were far too busy with a survey of the stables and the fields to conjecture on the lad's strange behavior. On completion of this, the tenant's wife graciously allowed them a tour through the farmhouse and Kate indicated the possible changes which could be made to expand and improve the residence.

"I think it can be done," Ralph announced, after they had thanked Mrs. Jollet and descended the front stairs. "Doesn't need to be too fancy or too big. Charity will love choosing the draperies and carpets and such. Have you . . ." Ralph was interrupted by the clatter of hooves in the drive. The brother and sister looked up to find Winterton approaching. He was leading the chestnut stallion.

"Good morning, Miss Montgomery, Ralph." He made a bow from the saddle and then dismounted. "I understand congratulations are in order, Ralph."

"Thank you, sir," Ralph murmured, his eyes on the chestnut.

"I have brought your wedding present. Can't have him eating his head off in my stables forever," Winterton grinned.

"M' father said you'd offered to see to the buying of the horse but that he'd refused. I had forgotten to tell him I wanted to purchase it," Ralph said, bemused.

Winterton kept his eyes on Ralph, unable to meet Kate's steady, fascinated gaze. "But I knew of your intention. I couldn't very well let Darfort have him."

Ralph was running his hands down the horse's legs. "You didn't have to go too high for him, did you?"

"You don't ask that of a wedding present," Winterton reminded him.

"No, no, of course not. Sorry," Ralph fumbled. "Must thank you. Very kind of you. Charity will be pleased."

Winterton laughed. "I doubt she will consider it the ideal present."

"Well, ordinarily that might be so," Ralph admitted. "But she knew I regretted not arranging for it." He shook Winterton's hand. "Very good of you. Much obliged."

"My pleasure," Winterton responded, and there followed an awkward moment before Ralph said, "I'll take him to the stables.'' He grasped the animal's bridle and left Kate and Winterton together.

"That was extremely thoughtful of you, my lord,'' Kate said softly. "Did the little Jollet boy come to tell you that Ralph was here?''

"I promised him half a crown,'' Winterton confessed, with a self-conscious grin. To avoid another clumsy silence he continued, "Walk with me a bit, please, and tell me of the plans for the farm now that Ralph is marrying.''

Kate took his arm and they strolled off aimlessly as she spoke of the arrangements which were being made. In her preoccupation she did not consider their direction until she found herself at the stream. She felt a blush rise to her cheeks and looked up at him inquiringly. "Did you do that on purpose?''

He met her eyes steadily. "Yes. I would have you overcome any embarrassment you feel about the incident.''

"I did not know, at the time . . . When I got home and saw myself in the mirror . . .'' Kate's voice drifted off in confusion, and her hand dropped from his arm.

"Sit here on the bank with me,'' Winterton urged gently, and Kate hesitantly obeyed. "When I watched you . . . swimming, you made an enchanting picture. No, do not blush. You were so determined and so free, I could not take my eyes from you. But when I came to your assistance and saw how revealing your . . . garment was, I spoke hastily from my own shock. Had I said nothing, you might never have discovered and been so . . . mortified. I was very clumsy, as I often am with you.''

"Why?''

"I beg your pardon?''

"Why are you often clumsy with me?" she asked frankly.

Winterton pulled a blade of grass and regarded it for a moment. Then he met her questioning eyes and answered honestly, "Because I am fond of you."

Kate nodded encouragingly. "I thought so, but why should that make you clumsy?"

A puzzled frown drew Winterton's dark brows together. When he did not speak Kate proceeded, "You are fond of Ralph and of Mr. Single, and you are not clumsy with them."

"How do you know?" he asked with ascerbity.

"Well, are you?"

"No, of course not."

"Perhaps you are clumsy with *women* you are fond of," Kate suggested mischievously.

"I am not fond of very many women," Winterton retorted, "and with those I am fond of, I am not clumsy."

"I see," Kate sighed. "It is only me, then?"

"Yes," he said firmly.

"That's interesting." Kate smoothed out the folds in her riding habit and gazed down to the stream. "Have I done something to make you wary of me?"

Winterton tapped his riding crop against his booted foot and replied exasperatedly, "You are mocking me, Miss Montgomery."

"You called me Kate the other day."

"Did I?"

"Yes, you said 'For God's sake, Kate, put some clothes on!' " Kate mimicked his horrified accents in the deepest voice she could manage, her eyes twinkling even as the blush again stained her face.

"You are provoking me, Kate," he said deliberately.

"I know, Lord Winterton." She kept her eyes firmly on her hands folded in her lap.

"Andrew. I should like to hear you call me Andrew."

"Very well, Andrew."

"Would you look at me, Kate?"

"Certainly, Andrew." She raised her eyes to his.

"The other day you started to describe your ideas on marriage. One ingredient was mutual respect. Are there others?"

"There must be a mutual . . . fondness. An attraction between the man and woman."

"Is there anything else?"

"I think it is easier if they are from approximately the same class. Do you not have ideas on marriage, L . . . Andrew?"

"I had not thought of it much until recently," he replied, his gaze on a tree across the stream.

"And what had you thought recently?"

"That I should like to marry you."

"This thought," Kate asked, "did you have it only after you saw me . . . swimming?"

Andrew swung around to face her, gripping her shoulders firmly. "Good God, no! How could you think so?"

"I merely wished to be sure," she replied in a small voice. "You have believed me capable of dishonor until quite recently, you see."

Andrew seemed to recollect himself. He dropped his hands from her shoulders and said slowly, "Even then I wanted to marry you, though I struggled with myself. I admit I used the swimming incident the other day as the easy way of inducing you to marry me."

"Yes," Kate retorted, "I thought that rather . . . clumsy of you."

"We have already established that I am clumsy with you, Miss Montgomery," he said stiffly.

"Do you suppose that is because you wish to marry me but cannot bring yourself to do so, Lord Winterton?" she asked sadly.

"I have asked you and you told me we should talk no more of it," Winterton pointed out, once again tapping his riding crop against his boot.

"It was unnecessary, given the circumstance."

"I have no wish to cause you further distress by pressing my suit."

"I should not feel the least bit distressed."

Andrew took her hands, his eyes locked with hers, and said carefully, "I have the greatest respect for you and I am fond of you. No, that is not altogether accurate. I . . . love you, Kate. And I dare say I shall become far less clumsy if you say you can return my regard."

"What you mean is that you will become quite dictatorial again if I do so," she speculated, a whimsical smile twitching her lips. "But there is nothing for it," she sighed. "I love you, Andrew."

"And you will marry me?" he asked, his pressure on her hands increasing.

"Yes, Andrew. I have developed a most unaccountable desire to see you in that incredible bed again."

"And I to teach you to swim, my love," he grinned. He pulled her into his arms and kissed her tenderly at first, and then in earnest. When at last they drew apart he said, "I had a letter from Charles today. He has requested my permission to wed your sister. I hope you will not allow that to prolong our engagement unduly."

"I should not dream of it," she responded breathlessly, a blush staining her cheeks.